MW00466662

Flannery O'Connor's *Why Do the Heathen Rage?*

Flannery O'Connor's *Why Do the Heathen Rage?*

A BEHIND-THE-SCENES LOOK AT A WORK IN PROGRESS

Jessica Hooten Wilson

Illustrated by Steve Prince, One Fish Studio

BrazosPress

a division of Baker Publishing Group
Grand Rapids, Michigan

© 2024 by Jessica Hooten Wilson

Cover art and interior illustrations © Steve Prince, One Fish Studio

The material from *Why Do the Heathen Rage?* is copyright Flannery O'Connor; all copyright renewed by Regina Cline O'Connor. Reprinted by permission of the Mary Flannery O'Connor Charitable Trust. All rights reserved.

Published by Brazos Press
a division of Baker Publishing Group
Grand Rapids, Michigan
www.brazospress.com

Printed in the United States of America

All rights reserved. No part of this publication may be reproduced, stored in a retrieval system, or transmitted in any form or by any means—for example, electronic, photocopy, recording—without the prior written permission of the publisher. The only exception is brief quotations in printed reviews.

Library of Congress Cataloging-in-Publication Data
Names: Wilson, Jessica Hooten, author. | O'Connor, Flannery. Why do the heathen rage.
Title: Flannery O'Connor's Why do the heathen rage? : a behind-the-scenes look at a
    work in progress / Jessica Hooten Wilson.
Description: Grand Rapids, Michigan : Brazos Press, a division of Baker Publishing
    Group, 2024. | Includes bibliographical references.
Identifiers: LCCN 2023022518 | ISBN 9781587436185 (cloth) | ISBN 9781493445028
    (ebook)
Subjects: LCSH: O'Connor, Flannery—Criticism and interpretation. | LCGFT: Literary
    criticism.
Classification: LCC PS3565.C57 Z95 2024 | DDC 813/.54—dc23/eng/20230512
LC record available at https://lccn.loc.gov/2023022518

The Author is represented by WordServe Literary Group, www.wordserveliterary.com.

Baker Publishing Group publications use paper produced from sustainable forestry practices and post-consumer waste whenever possible.

24   25   26   27   28   29   30   7   6   5   4   3   2   1

To my teacher Ralph C. Wood,
"the Dean of O'Connor Studies,"
to whom I owe the greatest of intellectual debts

And to the late Billy A. Sessions,
without whom this project would have never begun

CONTENTS

INTRODUCTION

When the train rolled to a stop in Milledgeville, Georgia, in December 1950, twenty-five-year-old Flannery O'Connor stumbled off the steel steps onto the familiar platform. The train station in Milledgeville still wears its tin roof like a slanted hat. The beams upholding the station are as dark as the trees flanking its sides. A row of six windows comprise two dozen panes, with two white French doors in the middle, composing the entrance. The building's red bricks are worn white in places from the heat. Struggling bushes separate the tracks and white gravel from the cement platform. Positioned at the edge of town, this simple structure waits for its people to come home.

Imagine the young O'Connor as she might have looked, clutching the banisters for support and muttering her thanks to the attendant as he set her bag beside her. Donning a beret tilted on her head and a threadbare winter coat, O'Connor was likely sweating from her besetting illness, lupus, despite the winter. From around the corner of the building, she would have heard a man call, "Mary Flannery!" Her head may have felt too heavy to lift, her arms numb from the effort of holding on to the wooden beam. Although Uncle Louis had known her all her life, he had not seen her in nine months, and she now appeared a shadow of her former self. The young girl who had flown off to Connecticut that past March to finish her first novel was returning as a "shriveled old woman."[1]

Flannery would spend that Christmas in Baldwin Memorial Hospital, as she had the year prior, when the doctors had operated on a floating kidney. In January, she would be transferred to Emory University Hospital in Atlanta, to be overseen by Dr. Arthur J. Merrill, a specialist whom friends and family credit for saving her life. Between heavy doses of cortisone, four shots a day of ACTH, and approximately ten blood transfusions, O'Connor must have felt like a science experiment gone wrong. She continued to work on her first novel, which she appropriately titled *Wise Blood*.

In March, after her release from the hospital, Flannery moved to Andalusia, a family farm near Milledgeville, which her mother ran. In her words, Flannery spent most of the day "languishing on [her] bed of semi affliction."[2] Her things were moved to the front room on the first floor of the house so she could avoid the stairs. She would spend the next nineteen years of her life in this home. While her mother Regina drove around the farm in her black Chevrolet checking on their twenty-two acres of roaming Holstein, Guernsey, and Jersey cows, Flannery spent the mornings facing away from the window, typing at her Royal, creating worlds not unlike her own but with the invisible brought high to the surface.

According to biographer Brad Gooch, the two women created an amiable routine.[3] Like a thirteenth-century nun, Flannery supposedly said her prime from *A Short Breviary* as the sun rose at 6 a.m. Then she would meet Regina for coffee in the kitchen, where they sometimes listened to the radio. For breakfast, O'Connor occasionally ate sharp cheddar shredded over her oatmeal. They habitually drove into town for 7 a.m. Mass at Sacred Heart Catholic Church, where they often sat in the fifth row. On either side of them, slats of sunlight streamed in and across from the large arched windows. When I visited the chapel, I was reminded of Hulga Hopewell declaring, "We are not our own light!"[4] Returning to Andalusia, Regina often toured the farm as Flannery wrote for the next three hours. They regularly lunched in downtown Milledgeville at the Sanford House, a beautiful white historic building with a columned double porch and balcony. In the afternoons, the O'Connor women might receive guests for tea on the front porch of the farm, where they would lounge in rocking chairs. For Flannery, the evenings were spent reading or corresponding with her friends and fans across the country.

In a span of ten years, O'Connor achieved great fame from her writing. In 1952, she published her first novel, *Wise Blood*. Over the next few years, she received the O. Henry Award three times—for "The Life You Save May Be Your Own," "Greenleaf," and "Everything That Rises Must Converge." Her first collection of short stories required three printings within the first few months of its release. Regionally, she received the Georgia Writers Association Literary Achievement Award, an Alumnae Achievement Award from her alma mater Georgia State College for Women, and the Georgia Writers Conference Literary Achievement Award. One of her short stories was adapted for the screen and starred Gene Kelly. Nationally, she received recognition from the Ford Foundation, the Best American Short Stories, and the American Academy of Arts and Letters. In 1960 she published her second novel, *The Violent Bear It Away*, and wrote a handful of other short stories. She died in 1964 at the age of thirty-nine.

Most people know O'Connor from her two short-story collections, her two novels, and her hundreds of letters, essays, and reviews, but she also left behind an unfinished third novel. Since she died so young, much of her work has been published posthumously, including her final set of short stories, *Everything That Rises Must Converge* (1965); her collection of essays *Mystery and Manners* (1969), edited by her friends Sally and Robert Fitzgerald; her *Complete Stories*, which received the first posthumous National Book Award (1971); her letters in *The Habit of Being* (1979); her book reviews in *The Presence of Grace* (1983); her interviews in *Conversations with Flannery O'Connor* (1987); her *Prayer Journal* (2013); and her college journal (2017). What has never been seen—by most of her readers—is her unfinished third novel, *Why Do the Heathen Rage?* In fact, until recently, many did not know that she had been working on a third novel when she died.

In 1970, the Georgia College and State University (GCSU) acquired her unorganized manuscripts and fragments of unfinished material. Initially, the drafts showed up in two large boxes, divided into approximately two hundred file folders. After several librarians and editors organized the material according to specific works and subdivided those manuscripts, the fragments of a third novel were found. The work had been tentatively titled *Why Do the Heathen Rage?* Its 378 typed and hand-edited pages were divided into twenty files, numbered 215 to 234.

Only a few years after O'Connor's mother Regina donated the unpublished pages to the library, a professor named Stuart Burns visited the archives, hoping to discover a complete work. His hopes were dashed when he discovered "no exciting, potentially publishable material."[5] Instead, he uncovered a frustrating collection of episodes—approximately a dozen—which are rehearsed and revised several times over. A decade later, scholar Marian Burns concurred with his assessment: "There is nothing approaching a proper novel in the unpublished manuscripts. There is only an untidy jumble of ideas and abortive starts, full scenes written and rewritten many times, several extraneous images, and one fully developed character."[6] Their conclusion remained consensus for the next few decades, as only three other scholars peered into the *Why Do the Heathen Rage?* manuscripts.[7]

Until now.

When I was a teenager trying to write fiction, Flannery O'Connor changed my life. At the time I was vacillating between my preference for dark and gory stories and the duty impressed upon me by my Christian parents to write nice, clean, happy stories. Over the summer between my sophomore and junior years of high school, I attended a Rhodes College program for talented and gifted writers. Although the campus looks like Cambridge University with its sandstone buildings covered with crawling ivy, Rhodes College is nestled in the heart of Memphis, Tennessee, across the street from the zoo. My dorm smelled slightly of monkey. I enrolled in a two-week fiction course. When I received feedback on my first story, the professor asked me to stay after class. He could see the dismay on my face as I processed all of his red marks.

"You have talent," he assured me. "Only you misuse it to turn out these parodies of *Saved by the Bell*. Why do you write such boring stories?"

As I tried not to cry in front of this forty-something PhD, I told him that my parents thought Christians should dwell on the good and the beautiful. I didn't know how much this well-meant advice was causing me to subvert my talents. Flannery would teach me that faith should never be used to sanitize fiction.

This professor handed me my first Flannery O'Connor story—"The Life You Save May Be Your Own."

"If you're a Christian," he said, "write like this." I followed his recommendation.

I imitated Flannery's story, and my heavily influenced short story won a National Scholastic Arts Award. I bought O'Connor's *Complete Stories* and pored over them from the first page to the last (only to later discover that the secret to reading O'Connor's stories is to read that collection backward, from the final few stories she wrote, such as "Revelation," back to "The Geranium"). Although I was never taught her work in college, I sought out professors in graduate school who would teach her to me, namely Ralph C. Wood, whom some call "the Dean of O'Connor Studies." Flannery's writing is as familiar to me as the Bible (to be fair, the Bible is much longer than her collected works). Even my children know Flannery and could point out her portrait in any lineup.

For me, the story of the publication of *Why Do the Heathen Rage?* begins with O'Connor's friend William A. "Billy" Sessions. I met Billy when he was seventy-nine and I was a newly minted PhD. We were both in Rome for the 2009 International Flannery O'Connor Conference, where he was one of half a dozen illustrious keynotes and I was an invisible graduate student presenting a chapter from my dissertation on O'Connor and Fyodor Dostoevsky. However, as a sophomore in college I had lived in Italy, and I still knew a bit of Italian as well as where to find the best restaurants in Rome, so I suddenly found myself playing tour guide to the keynote speakers. The first night of the event, I led them over cobblestone streets, across bridges, and down alleys into the dimly lit haven of Trastevere for dinner. Billy shuffled more than he walked. He wore a flat-top ivy cap that made him look like a tall Mickey Rooney (the octogenarian Rooney, not the former Andy Hardy persona). The rest of the party were O'Connor scholars about twenty to thirty years his junior and a dozen years my senior.

Billy had known Flannery since the 1950s, though she writes rather uncharitably about his garrulousness. When we met, Billy was working on O'Connor's biography, which he completed in 2016, months before he died, but which has not—as of 2023—been published. I had been a dedicated O'Connor fan since I was a fifteen-year-old struggling to write my own faithful but scandalous stories. That evening, surrounded by others who loved Flannery's writing as much as I did, I felt as if I was attending the greatest dinner party imaginable.

We ventured to La Cisterna, a restaurant that dates back to 1630 and is famous for the well beneath the street level. (Supposedly, the well inspired the writers of the Disney film *Fantasia*.) We sat in a circle, family style, and shared mounds of pasta with prosciutto and pecorino, and of course wine. Billy inquired about my dissertation and suggested that I take a look at O'Connor's unfinished novel: "It's her most Dostoevskian story." My eyes bulged from my head as I asked, "An unfinished novel?" I'm sure the same notions ran through my mind as had through Stuart Burns's so many decades before. I could hear fragments of others' conversations at the table. Someone was showing pictures of his new grandchild. I heard another person begin quoting Bruce Springsteen like his lyrics were poetry. But my life had just changed. An unfinished O'Connor novel that was inspired by Dostoevsky? I assured Billy I would be visiting the archives in Milledgeville within the year.

In December 2009 I took my first trip to the GCSU Special Collections, what would become one of many trips over the next decade. I remember my nerves upon entering that locked room, with its glass separation between scholars and the reception desk. No windows. No noise. Every scratch of a pencil or turn of a manuscript page seemed to echo in the stillness. If there was another scholar in the room, you could hear his stomach growl as lunch approached. I was allowed to bring my laptop in for notes, but no photographs were permitted. When the folders were brought out before me and placed on the table, I hardly dared to open them. The first folder was laid before me. The number "215" had been scratched on the front in pencil, and inside was the first page, which began with a note: "The following is a sample from a piece of fiction that goes under the working title, WHY DO THE HEATHEN RAGE?"[8] The first few pages were a replica of the same-titled short story published in *Esquire* in July 1963.

Before visiting the archives, I had read up on the short story. It begins with the Southern patriarch Tilman, who returns home from the hospital as an invalid after suffering a stroke, and it concludes with the final word "Jesus." O'Connor introduces all but one of her unfinished novel's main characters in this published excerpt: Mr. Tilman; Tilman's wife, the overbearing, hardworking mother of Walter; their son Walter, who is an educated loafer residing at home; their daughter Mary Maud, a schoolteacher; and Roosevelt, the Black field hand who becomes Tilman's companion and nurse after the stroke. The main character missing from the excerpt but featured in the novel in progress is Oona Gibbs.

In this opening excerpt, readers familiar with O'Connor will feel as though they've seen these characters before. When we're introduced to Walter, he sounds so similar to the heroes—or rather antiheroes— of O'Connor's other stories. The name of the character even switches in the lengthier manuscript between Julian (from "Everything That Rises Must Converge"), Asbury (from "The Enduring Chill"), and

Walter. Perhaps he is even more homeless, more lost and alienated, than any of these previous characters. Like Julian, his parent has suffered a stroke. Tilman's left eye twists inward, and Julian's mother is described with similar language: "One eye, large and staring, moved slightly to the left as if it had become unmoored."[9] Even in this short excerpt, Mrs. Tilman resembles Mrs. May (from "Greenleaf") and Mrs. McIntyre (from "The Displaced Person"), women who live to work rather than vice versa. And Mrs. Tilman misunderstands her son's reading habits the way Hulga's mother ("Good Country People") disapproves of her daughter's philosophical bent.

Esquire devoted its 1963 summer issue to writers' works in progress; O'Connor is featured beside Saul Bellow.[10] In the author's picture, she stares straight at the reader: a no-nonsense writer, her left hand supporting her head like an inverse Rodin statue. She wears a Peter Pan collar dress with a thin necklace, and she sports cat-eye glasses. Beneath her photo, the magazine mistyped her title—*Heathen* was made plural—and ran the caption, "Flannery O'Connor's first two novels were *Wise Blood* and *The Violent Bear It Away*; her third novel is as yet untitled, and she says it may be years before it's finished. This excerpt is from the beginning section." Apparently, even the title of the novel was unfinished.

The excerpt does not suggest much about O'Connor's intended plot, offer any opening or closing lines from the novel in progress, or hint at any larger structure, as if it were a microcosm of a whole. O'Connor knew the novel could take years to finish. While the genius of her first novel *Wise Blood* was evident to its first readers in 1952, when we read the short stories where the novel had its genesis, we see an immature writer figuring out her craft. The work took her at least five years to complete. Soon after its publication, O'Connor began *The Violent Bear It Away*, with which she fought "like a squirrel on a treadmill" for seven years before it was complete. She used the same phrase eight years later to express her frustration with her third novel: "I have been working all summer just like a squirril [*sic*] on a treadmill, trying to make something of Walter and his affairs and the other heathens that rage but I think this is not my material (don't like the word) but anyway I am committed to it for a spell at least."[11] Considering how much time these novels required of O'Connor, we may imagine she was years from finishing *Why Do the Heathen Rage?*

Aside from this brief selection, the rest of the unfinished material is similar to O'Connor's published stories. From "Comforts of Home," Sarah Ham (who calls herself Star Drake) seems closely related to Walter's New York correspondent, Sarah/Oona Gibbs. In an undeveloped episode, the character who would become O. E. Parker (from "Parker's Back") appears as the Tilmans' field hand Mr. Gunnels, who is covered with tattoos, including "a large head of Christ" on his back.[12] Finally, the manuscript possesses a handful of similarities to "Judgement Day," the story O'Connor revised from "The Geranium" in the final months of her life: Mr. Tilman has made eyeglasses for his servant Roosevelt, which parallels the Tanner and Coleman relationship, and Sarah's mother repeats Tanner's desire to be buried at home in the South after she dies.

Yet, was O'Connor trying to write a different story with this unfinished novel than she had before? The plot of the majority of the manuscript pages revolves around the developing relationship between Walter and Oona. In brief, Walter is a white Southern youth who writes letters to a social activist named Oona, who is driven by her spiritual inclinations, in which he pretends to be Black to test whether she postures more than she cares. The unfinished novel, in its dozen or so episodes, deals with political and social controversies, the civil rights movement, euthanasia, and poverty in ways O'Connor seems not to have attempted in her earlier fiction.

Flannery's characters are always more real to me than she is. I feel that, at every family reunion, I have encountered the grandmother from "A Good Man Is Hard to Find." The Misfit from that same story and Hazel Motes (the hero of *Wise Blood*) echo all my temptations and doubts about the church. Hulga from "Good Country People" sometimes stares back at me from the mirror. While boarding buses, I've observed that small, compact woman with a dress one size too small for her, a purple-flowered hat, and diminutive pumps, a lanky young man with her familial features sulking behind her, just as in "Everything That Rises Must Converge." In my mind's eye, I readily see the figures from "The Lame Shall Enter First": the scholarly looking gentleman driving his car, playing "Leave Me Do" loudly as his ten-year-old boy in the back seat pretends to be an astronaut, flying his soda can from one window to the next. I've stopped at gas stations across the South that smell of barbecue, like Red Sammy's ("A Good Man Is Hard to Find"). With trepidation, I've seen that questionable character, from the same story, in tight blue jeans and a Hawaiian shirt, a black hat, and glasses, pumping gas into his car with its dented hood. If you pay close enough attention, you may see a teenager with a clubfoot and no shoes scrounging through the aluminum trash bins ("The Lame Shall Enter First"). Or the woman with gold in her smile who walks hand in hand with a small boy in an oversize peacoat ("The River"). The characters of Flannery O'Connor inhabit my spaces and places as though they belong among me, and I've heard other readers share the same experience.

Yet, even for me, though I know her stories so well, it is hard to imagine Flannery herself moving among us. Every picture shows her stationary. I study photographs, but they all show different Flannerys: Frozen in a conga line at Yaddo with a shadowed face, she is a young girl whom anyone could be friends with, unpublished and approachable, ready for the world to know her name. At Andalusia farm, as a peacock taps the red dirt nearby, Flannery stands on the brick steps, smiling, a midlife woman leaning on aluminum crutches in a Sunday dress and pearls with frizzy hair and her signature glasses. There are paintings of Flannery that make her look more alive than her photos. Her self-portrait casts her as a Byzantine icon, holding a pheasant instead of a Bible, with her straw hat as a substitute halo. We never got to see her in old age, though other women in her family lived long lives. Her mother Regina was ninety-nine when she passed. Flannery's cousins have become nonagenarians. But Flannery's flesh succumbed to the red wolf at the young age of thirty-nine.

Unlike other writers whose incomplete novels have been published after their death, such as Ernest Hemingway, Ralph Ellison, or David Foster Wallace, who all died with an excess of unpublished papers from which editors could cut and splice, O'Connor left us only a handful of odd scenes. As much as we might wish that O'Connor had finished her third novel, we cannot invent what does not exist—a well-crafted, revised, full-length piece of fiction. To publish her unfinished work as a scholarly artifact would be unfaithful to O'Connor's intentions for the story. But if we create our own endings for the story, we must admit they are mere guesses and possibilities of what could have been.

If you visit the archives, the manuscript pages do not communicate to the reader a specific order of the episodes. There is no timeline of events. The various folders do not indicate which scenes should come first or last. My version of these pages comes from intersplicing sentences and paragraphs from the left-behind pages, making editorial choices about which words O'Connor meant to cut or keep, and presuming to show the best of what was left unfinished.

This book tells the story of the unfinished manuscript. I consider Flannery as she drafted the novel and what would have influenced her creation of the story: what was she reading, what news stories were making headlines, who was giving speeches on her new television. Spliced into these biographical passages are pieced-together episodes from the manuscript. The unfinished passages from O'Connor will be designated by the chapter title "Why Do the Heathen Rage?" and the sections that I drafted are bracketed separately. This way readers can distinguish between her material and my commentary. If O'Connor had lived, she would certainly have altered this material substantially. Ultimately, most of the decisions that I made were subjective and will meet with both approval and disapproval, as would any editor's choices. My highest aim was always to serve the artist and provide for the audience.

In trying to narrate how Flannery began this work but did not live to complete it, I feel as though I am relaying a story of one woman's failure. But, just like O'Connor's work, the full story includes the reader. When people finish reading her most anthologized short story, "A Good Man Is Hard to Find," they argue about whether the grandmother was saved at the conclusion. I'm quick to remind readers that Flannery did not set out to save the grandmother: she wanted to save her readers. Through her fiction, O'Connor vicariously points a gun at her imaginary readers and demands, "What do you believe?"

When Benny Andrews, the African American artist who illustrated "Everything That Rises Must Converge," decided to depict his illustrations of her story as "open-ended," he said that he was imitating O'Connor's story in doing so. In the story, the characters are "at the crossroads, but that's just where they are," Andrews writes in his afterword. "It is up to the reader of the story and the viewer of my artwork to look at the two Southerners [Black and white] and wonder, wonder, and hopefully wonder more."[13] Inspired by the way that Andrews dialogues through his art with O'Connor's story after her death, I asked the renowned artist Steve Prince to gloss the unfinished pages of O'Connor's novel. His art offers a way to go deeper in conversation with the material. Through his artistic engagement, Prince shows readers how to make O'Connor's words come alive in our space and time. We can continue from where she left off with our own responses and stories. After all, to be faithful to O'Connor's stories, especially her unfinished one, is to wonder about what happens *after* her last words. To let your story begin where hers left off. We can never know what she intended, but like Andrews, we can read and wonder.

Sticks and Stones

Why Do the Heathen Rage?

THE PORCH SCENE[1]

The girl descended on them a little before noon, rattling up the corrugated clay road in a small red automobile that raised a trail of pink dust behind it.

At ten the previous morning Walter had been in his room, furiously typing a letter, which was intended to bring her on. "The only way you will know," he wrote, "is to come. Get one look. You won't stay. You don't know your right hand from your left. I want you to come. Meadow Oaks is waiting for you. It's the place for your revelation. You'll stay just long enough to look once and then you'll turn and run. None of that bunk about holding my hand to your cheek." He stopped and gazed at his hands spread out on the typewriter. He continued typing, "My hand is black. It would burn a hole through your face." His hands were not black but white, or rather pink, naturally florid and speckled palely. The sun seldom saw them. He lifted one of them and rubbed it over the bald spot at the top of his head, down one of his steaming cheeks and under the fold of his chin. Then he began to type again.

After a moment, he paused and gazed through the window near him, out over the side meadow, where Eustis was on the tractor, mowing yellow weeds. The Negro shouted a song to the Lord over the rumble of the machine, flung it out as if the Lord were sitting forward on the throne of heaven with his hand cupped to his ear to catch the words. The sight of him seemed to intensify Walter's efforts. He returned to his letter, sweat pearling on his face. He was making love through the mail under an assumed name and an assumed race to a woman he had never seen. His eyes, grey blue behind his thick glasses, appeared to sweat also. There was in them a kind of agonized impatience.

While Walter was typing, his father, T. C. Tilman, was being wheeled out onto the front porch. This was the second anniversary of Tilman's stroke. Every morning after breakfast, Roosevelt, his attendant, brought him to sit for the rest of the morning, where he could glare across the lawn at the four oaks that gave Meadow Oaks its name.

Around the corner of the house, just under his window, Walter's mother was on her hands and knees in the rose bed, digging. Nothing could be seen of her but her feet in black oxfords and over the top of a rose bush, her red and yellow sun hat. She was planting a tin can with a hole in the bottom of it beside each bush. Water poured in the can went directly to the roots of the plant and was not wasted. Walter's typing came from directly above. It was a noise distinctly unpleasant to her like the swarming of bees in a chimney. He was not writing anything worthwhile, only letters. He wrote letters to people he did not know and ignored those he knew.

She got up from the rose bed and dusted her knees. She was a small grey-haired woman, compact and neat. She might, like the trowel she had been digging with, have been designed for some special purpose. She walked around to the front of the house, looking critically at the shrubbery as she went. It was coated with dust from the road. She mounted the steps and sat down in a rocker on the porch with Tilman.

Tilman was not quite of the social stuff Walter's mother was, but common sense had dictated that she marry him. She had elevated his taste very little. He would have been content to eat off plated ware instead of the Grandstaff silver, and in public as in private, he scratched where he itched. His face was common as a clay road. At sixty, he still had a shock of thick yellowish white hair. The Grandstaff men lost their hair and their money, but they retained the intangibles. Tilman had bought the Grandstaff place just in time to save it from the sheriff.

Once or twice during the morning, she sat down with Tilman and asked some foolish question to give him the illusion he was running the place. She took off her sun hat and ran her arm across her forehead. Her mouth pursed at the sight of his attendant, a large, very black, apparently boneless Negro, who sat facing him in a straight chair tilted against the rail. His cheek and open mouth rested on the shoulder of his white orderly's jacket. His feet lay together sole to sole, and he slept soundlessly. The normal way of things, her expression said. While the mistress works, the servant rests. As sorry as he was, she was thankful for him. He did what had to be done for Tilman.

"Don't you think it's time to plow the bottom?" she asked.

"It's too wet to plow," rasped Tilman, as if any fool would know it was too wet to plow. He sat with his brown felt hat pulled forward over his face at the same sharp angle as his nose. His blue pajamas hung down an inch or so below his grey trouser legs. His stick lay across his knees. From time to time, with his usable hand, he thumped it on the floor as if to make sure there was still something solid underneath him. Tilman was not aware that this was the second anniversary of his stroke. He played time now like an accordion. Whatever way he pushed, it went.

She had had the bottom plowed already, the day before, regardless of the drought. What was run, she ran because Walter, whose job it should have been, was no help. He was a total loss. As soon as the doctor assured her that Tilman would never be the man he had once been, she had begun to make changes. First, she restored the name of the place to Meadow Oaks. Thirty years ago, when Tilman took over the mortgage, he had cut "Coon Farm" in aluminum and decorated the sign with a miniature colored boy eating watermelon. This abomination he placed atop the mailbox at the edge of the highway. She left him and stayed gone until he took it down—three weeks—but

her victory was temporary. He had the tasteless emblem transferred
to business stationery and the name stuck.

In the nineteenth century, when the Grandstaffs owned it, the
place had been called Meadow Oaks. Beyond the front lawn and the
red dirt road that came in from the highway was a broad meadow.
On it, in a half circle, stood four giant oaks. The oaks had been mammoth even in the Grandstaffs' time. The Grandstaffs had called them
Matthew, Mark, Luke, and John. She had lived in dread for thirty
years that they would fall to Tilman, that one morning he would
walk out onto the front porch, look across the lawn and the road
and out into the meadow and see them for the first time, standing
immense, murmuring, mysterious. He would sense something larger
than himself and in his outrage, he would realize instantly that they
were potential lumber, sufficient to panel an office or put up a Jiffy
Home. Miraculously, it had not happened. He cut timber everywhere
else, but for all those years, he had appeared to notice those four oaks
no more than he noticed the ground beneath his feet, and now she
was safe. Nobody cared what he noticed now. He had not seen the
iron marker she had had cast for the mailbox. It said MEADOW OAKS
in modified Old English capitals.

"Won't be able to plow for another week," Tilman said.

She nodded, for there was no need now ever to oppose him. Once
during his second month at home from the hospital, he had showed
alarming signs of improvement. She had not hesitated. She had gone
to the bank and borrowed the money to have the house completely
repaired and painted. They did not know when the house had been
built, but to judge from the way it was put together, it was old enough
to count. The beams were joined with wooden pegs two feet long,
the columns, though narrow, were hand-carved, the front steps were
double and went down in two broken wings to old brick walks that
led off at either side.

Inside it was dignified and drafty, furnished by her family belong-
ings, except Tilman's television and a modern kitchen, which she had
installed. Tilman's plan had been to allow the house to waste away

until it was no longer habitable, and then to wreck it and put up a brick house such as he had admired in city suburbs, one low to the ground and with a large plate glass window in front. His improvement had not lasted, but if worse had come to worst, and he had recovered, the house at least would have been ahead.

Tilman always had plenty of money or knew where he could lay hands on it, but after his stroke, she found that there was none and that she was in debt. She had thought that this would bring out Walter's sense of responsibility. It had not. Nothing had any effect on him. He seemed now to be in the best of health and spirits, but in a perverse sort of way. He was not interested in work or in women or in money or in liquor or in politics. He read a great deal, but what was the use of improving a mind that you didn't use?

Walter's typewriter, which had been silent for a few minutes, began to clatter again in the upper distance. Tilman jerked his head in the direction of the noise. A fierce light came into his left eye, which, from the stroke, turned inward slightly. "He ought to be plowing," he said. "He ain't too good to plow."

She only sighed. The sound of the typewriter was a sign to her of some deep-rooted failure in her life, and to Tilman, in whose life there were no failures, of the fact that Walter was no damn good.

"He's a scholar," she said. She had arrived at this term for his semi-occupation as a genteel shield for his peculiarities. She preferred it to "intellectual." She thought of a scholar as someone who knew too much but remained a gentleman with it all. An intellectual just knew too much.

To Tilman a scholar meant a schoolboy. A diller, a dollar, a ten o'clock scholar. "He's a goddamned idler, that's what he is," Tilman said.

"He contributes," she said bitterly. "You can't say he doesn't contribute to the expenses." To keep himself in the necessities and to pay her board, Walter tended a liquor store on Highway 22 every night from six to twelve. Mrs. Tilman did not like to speak of this; she did not even like to think of it. Her friends, if they happened to drive by that place at night, beheld Walter inside the glass box garishly lit with bands of red and blue and green electric light, poised against a rich background of bottles. He sat in a straight chair tilted against the counter, reading with intense concentration. Outside were the woods and the night. Except on Friday and Saturday when there was an influx of Negro customers, business was light. Walter who had the brains to be a lawyer or a doctor or an engineer and to excel at whatever he did, considered it an ideal job.

"Selling *stamped* liquor to n——s," Tilman said, as if this were as far as a fool could go.

"It's the times," she said, "it's the whole world." She looked dolefully out over the meadow where the four oaks stood guard. They stood like a vanguard of the army of woods, which ranged behind them in a vast circle, row upon row until the last grey line touched the horizon. Just to look at the place, no one would know that the world had affected it. Except for the presence of various pieces of machinery, it looked almost the way it had looked in her father's time, but between her father's time and now, something had happened to make people's children go crazy. Walter was not incapable of working. He had worked to put himself through school because Tilman had refused to send him. "We should have insisted he stick with law," she said, "or if he had to switch, switch to something he could do when he got out, not just think about, but then we weren't paying for it. That's where we made our mistake," she said, looking sharply at Tilman, "not paying for it—then we would have had some say-so." Plainly it had been Tilman who had refused to pay for it.

"I've been sick two weeks," he announced abruptly as if this revelation had just been vouchsafed him. Then he corrected himself. "No, I've been home from the hospital two weeks, in the hospital three weeks. Didn't like it a damn bit," he added. He sensed nothing amiss. Had he been home three weeks or had he been sick three weeks? Anyway, he could look around him and see that common sense had been knocked cold in his absence. She had painted the house, though the damn house was ready to fall down.

Tilman had had his stroke in the state capital, where he had gone on business, and he had stayed two weeks in the hospital there. He did not remember his arrival home by ambulance, but his wife did. She had sat for two hours on the jump seat at his feet, gazing fixedly at his face. Only his left eye, twisted inward, seemed to harbor his former personality. It burned with rage. The rest of his face was prepared for death. Justice was grim and she took satisfaction in it when she found it. It might take just this ruin to wake Walter up.

By accident both children had been at home when they arrived. Mary Maud had driven in from school, not realizing that the ambulance was behind her. She got out—a large woman of thirty with a round childish face and a pile of thin carrot-colored hair that seeped about in an invisible net on top of her head—kissed her mother, glanced at Tilman and gasped; then, grim-faced but flustered, marched behind the rear attendant, giving him high-pitched directions on how to get the stretcher around the curve of the front steps. Exactly like a school teacher, her mother thought. School teacher all over. As the forward attendant reached the porch, Mary Maud said sharply in a voice used to controlling children, "Get up, Walter, and open the door!"

Walter was sitting on the edge of a chair, absorbed in the proceedings, his finger folded in the book he had been reading before the ambulance came. He got up and held open the door and while the attendants carried the stretcher across the porch, he gazed, obviously fascinated, at his father's face. "Glad to see you back, capt'n," he said and raised his hand in a sloppy salute.

Tilman's enraged left eye appeared to include him in its vision but he gave no sign of recognition.

Roosevelt, who from now on would be nurse instead of yard man, stood inside the door, waiting. He had put on the white coat that he was supposed to wear for occasions. He peered forward at what was on the stretcher. The bloodshot veins in his eyes swelled. Then, all at once, tears glazed them and glistened on his black cheeks like sweat. Tilman made a weak rough motion with his good arm. It was the only gesture of affection he had given any of them. The Negro followed the stretcher to the back bedroom, snuffling as if someone had hit him.

Mary Maud went in to direct the stretcher bearers. Walter and his mother remained on the porch. "Close the door," she said, "you're letting flies in." She had been watching him all along, searching for some sign in his big, bland face that some sense of urgency had touched him, some sense that now he had to take hold, that now he had to do something, anything—she would have been glad to see him make a mistake, even make a mess of things if it meant that he was doing something—but she saw that nothing had happened. His eyes were on her, glittering just slightly behind his glasses. He had taken in every detail of Tilman's face, he had registered Roosevelt's tears, Mary Maud's confusion, and now he was studying her to see how she was taking it. She yanked her hat straight on her head, seeing by his eyes that it had slipped toward the back of her head.

"You ought to wear it that way," he said. "It makes you look sort of relaxed-by-mistake."

She made her face as hard as she could make it. "The responsibility is yours now," she said in a harsh, final voice.

He stood there with his half smile and said nothing. Like an absorbent lump, she thought, taking everything in, giving nothing out. She might have been looking at a stranger using the family face. He had the same noncommittal lawyer's smile as her father and grandfather, set in the same heavy jaw, under the same Roman nose; he had the same eyes that were neither blue nor green nor grey; his skull would soon be bald like theirs. Her eyes became even harder. "You'll have to take over and manage this place," she said, "if you want to stay here."

The smile left him. He looked at her once hard, his expression empty, and then beyond her out across the meadow, beyond the four oaks and the black distant tree line into the vacant afternoon sky. "I thought it was home," he said, "but it don't do to presume."

Her heart constricted. She had an instant's revelation that he was homeless. Homeless here and homeless anywhere. "Of course, it's home," she said, "but somebody has to take over. Somebody has to make these Negroes work."

"I can't make Negroes work. That's about the last thing I'm capable of."

"I'd tell you everything to do," she said.

"Ha!" he said. "That you would." His half smile returned. "Lady," he said, "you're coming into your own. You were born to take over. If the old man had had his stroke ten years ago, we'd all be better off. You could have run a wagon train through the Badlands. You could stop a mob. You're the last of the nineteenth century, you're . . ."

"Walter, you're a man. I'm only a woman."

"A woman of your generation," Walter said, "is better than a man of mine."

Her mouth drew into a tight line of outrage and her head trembled almost imperceptibly. "I would be ashamed to say it," she whispered.

Walter dropped into the chair he had been sitting in and opened his book. A sluggish-looking flush settled on his face. "The only virtue of my generation," Walter said, "is that it ain't ashamed to tell the truth about itself." He was already reading. Her interview was at an end.

She remained standing there, rigid, her eyes on him in stunned disgust. Her son. Her only son. His eyes and his skull belonged to the family face, but underneath them was a different kind of man from any she had ever known. There was no innocence in him, no rectitude, no conviction of either sin or election. The man she saw courted good and evil impartially and looked at so many sides of every question that he could not move, he could not work, he could not even make n——s work. Any evil could enter that vacuum. God knows, she thought and caught her breath, God knows what he might do!

He had not done anything. He was twenty-eight now and, so far as she could see, nothing occupied him but trivia. He had the air of a person who is waiting for some big event and can't start any work because it would only be interrupted. Since he was always idle, she had thought perhaps he wanted to be an artist or a philosopher or something, but this was not the case. He did not want to write anything with a name. He amused himself writing letters to people he did not know and to the newspapers. Under different names and using different outlandish personalities, he wrote to strangers. It was a peculiar, small, contemptible vice. Her father and her grandfather had been moral men, but they would have scorned small vices more than great ones. They knew who they were and what they owed to themselves. It was impossible to tell what Walter knew or what his views were on anything. He read books that had nothing to do with anything that mattered now. Often she came behind him and found some strange underlined passage in a book he had left somewhere and she would puzzle over it for days. One passage that she found in a book he had left lying on the upstairs bathroom floor stayed with her ominously.

"Love should be full of anger," it began, and she thought, well, mine is. It went on, "Since you have already spurned my request, perhaps you will listen to admonishment. What business have you in your father's house, O you effeminate soldier? Where are your ramparts and trenches, where is the winter spent at the front lines? Listen! the battle trumpet blares from heaven and see how our General marches fully armed, coming amid the clouds to conquer the whole world. Out of the mouth of our King emerges a double-edged sword that cuts down everything in the way. Arising finally from your nap, do you come to the battlefield? Abandon the shade and seek the sun."

She turned back in the book to see what she was reading. It was a letter from a St. Jerome to a Heliodorus, scolding him for having abandoned the desert. A footnote said that Heliodorus was one of the famous group that had centered around Jerome at Aquileia in 370. He had accompanied Jerome to the Near East with the intention of cultivating a hermitic life. They had separated when Heliodorus continued on to Jerusalem. Eventually he returned to Italy, and in later years he became a distinguished churchman as the bishop of Altinum. This was the kind of thing he read—something that made no sense for now. Then it came to her, with an unpleasant jolt, that the General with the sword in his mouth, marching to do violence, was Jesus.

She found this notion extremely unpleasant. Everything his generation took to had to be ugly—ugly pictures, ugly music, and now it occurred to her, an ugly Jesus. She suddenly felt bone-tired, unable to summon the strength of will to call her rage. The trouble with the world was it never worked until it was exhausted. It always had energy left over to want something ugly. She envisioned herself with a whip in her hand, driving the world to work until it dropped. Work and sleep was all it was fit for. The only sin was to stop work long enough to want something ugly.

She never thought about Jesus herself but her sense of election had never failed her. She herself was not religious. She thought of others above herself, always did the right thing, without any fuss, and that was that. One thing she had always prayed was that if her children were religious, they would not be religious in a bad sense, that they would not be too religious, that they would not have warped personalities. As it was they were not religious at all, at least Mary Maud was not. Walter read books like this, but she did not believe that Walter was either. Tilman was the only religious member of the family. She did not know why Walter should read stuff like this except that if you were a scholar you read antiquated things.

"I'll stay in bed one more week," Tilman said. "A cold lasts three weeks if you treat it and twenty-one days if you let it alone."

She felt a presence at the door behind them and turned her head. Walter stood there with a letter in his hand to take to the mailbox. He might have slept in his clothes. He wore dirty moccasins and khaki pants and a plaid shirt hanging out. She looked closer at him to see if he had shaved. One thing she would not tolerate was a beard. He had shaved but nonetheless he looked ape-like. His slump was becoming more and more pronounced.

She stood up decisively. "I want Roosevelt to take up some peony plants for me," she said. "They're getting too much sun. You stay with your daddy until he gets back." Whenever she could interrupt his leisure and require something of him, she did it on principle.

Walter's brows rose in annoyance but he looked cornered.

Tilman's nostrils flared. "Let him do it!" he cried, pointing his cane at Walter. "That n—— needs his rest. He was up half the night with me."

"He gets more rest than anybody I know—black or white," she said. "If anybody around here needs rest, it's me. Roosevelt!" she said, raising her voice.

The Negro lifted his head slowly and opened one bloodshot eye and looked at nothing, sullenly, as if he had been warned in his sleep that on awakening he would have her to contend with. They were old enemies. Incompatible from the first moment they had seen each other.

"Go get your shovel," she said. "We're going to move some plants."

"Shovel broke," he muttered, still speaking to nothing.

"Go get any shovel you can find," she said in a flat even voice, "broken or unbroken."

He got up and moved off the porch.

She turned to Tilman. "Now you and Walter can enjoy each other until he gets back," she said with a glint of grim pleasure in her eye.

Walter lowered himself to the top step and sat there tapping the envelope on his thumbnail. He gazed across the lawn and out toward the meadow where the four oaks stood.

Tilman glared down at the top of his head. "I won't have people treating my n—— like a dog," he said in a high voice. "He needs his rest. *He* works!"

He would have swapped Walter any day for Roosevelt who was a half-wit. A n—— half-wit is always preferable to a white one. He would have swapped either of his children, or both, for the Negro. He envisioned a scene with his Maker in which he got this straight. They met at a crossroads, each in his pale, mud-spattered car, and pulled alongside. Neither got out; each measured the other with his eyes. Presently, Tilman said, "You can have the two you stuck me with. I want the n——," and the mirror image of himself in the other car, eyeing him inscrutably from beneath the brim of his brown felt hat, said, "If you want that black scoundrel, you can have him, but don't try to unload the other two on me."

"You want anything mailed?" Walter asked, becoming conscious of the old man over him, demanding attention.

Tilman eyed the letter savagely. With an effort that made him rigid he piped, "No!" He had not had the use of his right arm for two weeks and the fool asked him if he had wanted anything mailed. He made an effort again and piped, "No!" a second time. Then it occurred to him that Walter was only making conversation, that he didn't even know what he had asked. The thought that this big fat lump of learning felt sorry for him completed his rage. The letter was in an airmail envelope. The idiot mailed all his letters in an airmail envelope as if they were of the greatest importance. He toiled not, neither did he spin, but he mailed his letters in airmail envelopes.

Walter looked up at the sky, squinting. It was a pale even noncommittal blue. "Don't look like it'll rain today," he said.

The old man's jaw slid forward. "There's not a cloud in the sky," he wheezed. "Any fool would know it's not going to rain." The seasons could all be the same and this idiot would not be affected. He made himself rigid and with a tremendous control of all his muscles, he leaned forward and quavered, "When are you going to work?" His heart beat as if he had lifted a keg of nails, and he subsided panting.

"Working on something now," Walter murmured.

"Ought to been a damn postman," Tilman said. In a second, he corrected himself. "Too lazy to be a damn postman."

His wife appeared at the edge of the lawn with Roosevelt behind her, slumped over an apple crate and a shovel that he was carrying. He set it down at her feet and she began pointing with the trowel at the plants she wanted dug up.

"That's no yard n——," Tilman grumbled. "You ought to be doing that!" He swung the wheelchair nearer to Walter with his good arm. "When I was your age I had two sawmills. I worked."

Walter kept turning the airmail letter over in his hand. It was addressed to Miss Oona Gibbs, Fellowship Farm, Rocky Branch, Tennessee.

"You don't have any bidnis," Tilman said, "that a four-cent stamp wouldn't get it there." He wheeled his chair close enough to see the name on the envelope. Miss Somebody. A woman would have to be ten kinds of a fool to see anything in Walter. In a minute, he made out the address. At first his mind registered nothing. Then something about the name, the very sound of Fellowship Farm began to fill him with rage.

Tilman sat before the television for an hour every evening before supper and glared at the news of the day. Each day's news blended into a continuous affront like a raucous song made up of senseless insults. Every evening he recharged his battery of rage before the machine. Fellowship Farm struck a raw familiar chord in him though he could not identify it. His eyes moved balefully from the bald spot at the back of Walter's head, down the bulging blue plaid shirt, over the khaki-covered knees to the dirty yellow moccasins that looked like a giant's baby shoes. This lump of lard was his son. This scholar! This liquor salesman! This philosopher! This pink-spectacled damn fool that was writing to Fellowship Farm! Suddenly what Fellowship Farm was came through to him.

"Why don't you go there!" he cried in a thin voice that strained to be a roar. "Why don't you clear out of here and go live with those sons of apes?" He thrust his cane into Walter's ribs and the letter went sailing down the steps.

Walter jumped to retrieve it.

"Damned radicals! Liars!" Tilman wheezed. His chair was coming forward as if he would wheel it off the porch.

Walter caught the letter and reached the top step again in time to grab the chair with both hands.

"Communists!" Tilman hissed into his face.

"They're Baptists!" Walter said and smiled wickedly at the old man. "Just like you. Baptists run it. I just happen to know this woman who's visiting there. They're living like the gospels say live."

"Anybody calls himself a Baptist, that don't make him one!" Tilman cried.

Walter continued to smile at him, but his mind had returned to Oona Gibbs. He sat down on the steps again, confident that the letter would bring her on.

KOINONIA

Fellowship Farm is a thinly veiled allusion to Koinonia Farm—
koinōnia means "fellowship" in Greek—which was founded in
Americus, Georgia, in 1942, only two hours from O'Connor's
home in Milledgeville. It began making headlines in 1956 after
its founder Clarence Jordan sponsored two African American
students who sought admission to the University of Georgia. In
1957 O'Connor's friends, Father McCown and Tom and Louise
Gossett, invited her to join them on a visit to the community.
She declined, relating to her dear friend Betty Hester that the
trip would be "inconvenient in more ways than one." Yet she
writes, "I wish somebody would write something sensible about
Koinonia." While O'Connor agrees that the community "should
be allowed to live in peace," she disagrees with the hagiographic
write-ups about its mission.[1] Although she had not yet been
working on *Why Do the Heathen Rage?*, O'Connor shows that
she attended to the news about Koinonia with mixed feelings
of support and anxiety.

In 1957 Dorothy Day, the founder of the Catholic Worker
Movement, a group primarily located in New York, attempted
to show her solidarity with the interracial farming community.
She boarded a Greyhound bus and traveled down to Georgia
during the final two weeks of Lent. On her third night at Koinonia, Day and her friend Elizabeth sat watch for the farm, which
had been under attack since Jordan's stance for integration had
become more public.

The two women sat in a parked station wagon, listening to cicadas whirring and spinning in the air. An oak tree spread its arms so wide and high it cast centuries of leaves in a cover that hid the stars. Day and Elizabeth began to sing vespers to one another in low voices. Day was sixty, with a heavy chest, a small waist, and a determined chin. She often wore her hair pulled back beneath a handkerchief; her dress was homespun. Nothing could be heard but the sound of their low-sung hymns and the buzz of the insects overhead until a sudden spattering of sound: gunshots popped and cracked through the stillness. Their car was peppered with gunfire by an unseen passerby. After the assailants shot at the women, they accelerated with full force and raced away. Neither woman was hurt. Neither ducked. Neither moved. They sat immobilized by fear. Within seconds, their song had been hushed by violence.

Thankfully, neither Day nor her friend was injured in the attack. O'Connor's response to the news, which she read from Day's column in the *Catholic Worker*, was, by her own lights, "ugly and uncharitable—such as: that's a mighty long way to come to get shot at." Yet O'Connor writes in the very next sentence, "I admire her very much." She then muses, "I hope that to be of two minds about some things is not to be neutral."[2] O'Connor expresses these two divergent perspectives in *Why Do the Heathen Rage?*

In a few of the manuscripts, Oona's group actually runs Fellowship Farm and is located either in Osagoola, New York,[3] or Rocky Branch, Tennessee.[4] However, "Friendship, Inc." becomes the group's designation in the letters in which Oona describes her mission.[5] Despite the similarity between Friendship, Inc., and Koinonia, from which O'Connor likely drew inspiration, O'Connor does not seem to be parodying the group. On the one hand, Walter is aggravated by Oona's intrusion into Southern politics, but on the other hand, he agrees with her theoretically about the need for social justice. He defends the farm to his father as an example of Christian living.

Walter's parents express the alternative point of view; both are outraged at the existence of Fellowship Farm or Friendship, Inc. They associate such groups with Bolshevism, which historically was an accusation that Jordan himself faced when he defended Koinonia.[6] For O'Connor, Koinonia was a reality that confronted her assumptions about gospel living. As Charles Marsh explains it, Koinonia Farm embodied "that abrasive quality that the apostle Paul had described as the willingness to appear freakish and peculiar."[7] While O'Connor may have wanted to embrace the ideas that led to Koinonia's founding, she seems to doubt in her letters whether she herself would be comfortable living in a similar fashion. This apparent divide between her cognitive assertions and actual practice, especially with regard to Christianity and the civil liberties of African Americans, is evidenced in O'Connor's fiction and letters from the last few years of her life.

In O'Connor's restored bedroom there is only one piece of art set high on the bookcases: a portrait of Louise Hill, the African American woman who cared for the O'Connors' home. It was painted by O'Connor's friend Robert Hood and given to her as a gift. The portrait is impressionistic; many of the colors appear to melt into one another. If you stare at it for long, the face begins to look like an icon.

I picture Flannery in this museum-curated version of her bedroom, without the orange crate beneath her desk with its assortment of unorganized papers, her newspaper clippings scattered across her bed.

"Types faster than I can think," she laments aloud, echoing her letters.

"What's that?" a voice says from the other side of the armoire. Louise might be dusting the portrait of herself again this morning, feigning that the room needs cleaning.

"Louise, my mornings are nonnegotiable," Flannery might snap. Her glasses pinch the bridge of her nose and her eyes dart back and forth over her near-empty page, trying to remember the thought she has lost. Every day that she could (even on Sundays in the final years of her illness), Flannery worked from 9 a.m. to noon, hoping for no interruptions.

According to Flannery, Louise often came in to dust her own portrait and admire her image. There was a gold crucifix on the wall behind Flannery that would have been figuratively boring into her neck. The hanging Christ on the cross demands that we be charitable, but sometimes all we can muster is suppressed wrath over wasted reflections.

SEQUEL TO "THE ENDURING CHILL"

Readers can observe similarities between O'Connor herself and the hero of her third novel, Walter Tilman—sitting at home, heads full of schooling, not quite a fit with those around them. Most in Milledgeville still knew O'Connor as "Regina's daughter who writes." When the president of her alma mater introduced her at a function, he described O'Connor as "one who had been on and off the best-seller lists."[1] No prophet is respected in their hometown.

Since she had written "The Enduring Chill" more than five years earlier, O'Connor had some idea that she wanted to tell the continuation of Asbury's story. In "The Enduring Chill," Asbury is a young artist who returns home to the South from New York because he fears his death is near. The reality is that Asbury has undulant fever from drinking raw milk at the dairy; this sickness came about because of his pride, his show of revolt against his mother's restrictions, and his attempt to prove to the two African American workers that he, as an educated man from the North, had progressed above racial divides. His sickness, along with a couple of humiliating conversations with a priest and a local doctor, move Asbury to a point of revelation regarding his own smallness. Amid his fever, Asbury stares at a water stain on his ceiling that seems to come to life and descend upon him to upturn his whole world.

O'Connor wrote later, "I don't think of conversion as being once and for all and that's that. I think once the process is begun and continues that you are continually turning inward toward God and away from your own egocentricity and that you have to see this selfish side of yourself in order to turn away from it."[2] But how to write about a convert? How to depict the "long obedience in the same direction"?[3] Such saintly behavior makes for undramatic copy. O'Connor had spent a career depicting epiphanies, moments of grace that intrude upon the unsuspecting, or hounds of heaven that chase down and maul the unrepentant sinner. Now she wanted to try a new direction. In 1963, O'Connor confessed to Sister Mariella Gable, "I've reached the point where I can't do again what I know I can do well, and the larger things that I need to do now, I doubt my capacity for doing."[4]

The inkling to write a novel as a sequel to "The Enduring Chill" came to her in December 1957. O'Connor writes to her friend Betty Hester, "I have it in mind to take Asbury further maybe into other stories."[5] The next year, she continues this train of thought in a letter to Ted Spivey: "I've thought maybe there is enough in these characters [from "The Enduring Chill"] to make a novel of them sometime but it would be a novel with this story as the first chapter and the rest of it would be concerned with the boy's efforts to live with the Holy Ghost, which is a subject for a comic novel of no mean proportions."[6] Although O'Connor had not yet completed *The Violent Bear It Away*, she held fast to this idea of continuing Asbury's story. In May 1959, she informs another friend, Maryat Lee, of her desire to "write more about Asbury": "Asbury and his mamma are good for something else but I haven't decided what."[7]

After months spent rewriting the opening paragraph almost a dozen times, about all that Flannery has accomplished is to rename Asbury. "The name Asbury don't interest me," she admits.[8] In the manuscript pages, Asbury is sometimes Charles and sometimes Julian, but most often, Flannery names her primary character Walter. While some of her characters are named with heavy allusions or Dickensian monikers, her source for names may have been as simple as the Memory Hill Cemetery that she and her mother visited often. In addition to their family's graves, most notably that of Flannery's father Edward, "Asbury Church" is buried there, as are "John Wesley" and "Charles Wesley" and others who make cameos in her fiction.[9]

However, she probably drew Walter's name from the saints and religious figures of the past, such as Walter the Penniless, Hubert Walter the twelfth-century archbishop of Canterbury, Walter of Coutances, Walter of Coventry, Saint Walter of Pontoise, or Walter Hilton, the fourteenth-century English mystic. The year before Flannery began writing her new novel, she read *The Medieval Mystics of England*, which included Walter Hilton's *The Scale of Perfection*. Hilton wrote letters to laypeople about spiritual questions, particularly the relationship between the active life and the contemplative life.[10] In a handwritten note on the manuscript, O'Connor has Walter call himself a "secular contemplative."[11] Of course, the trajectory may have been for Walter's secular contemplation to be unveiled as Christian contemplation.

Thankfully, after some chastising by fellow Catholic novelist J. F. Powers, O'Connor had broken free from her habit of killing off all her characters, so she had some material to work with. Powers called her on this "embarrassment," in her words, after he read "Greenleaf." She responded, "I guess I'll have to resurrect Mrs. May as Mrs. Somebody-else and start over."[12] She understood him to mean that she "should have left [the character] alive so that [she] could write a novel about her."[13] A year later, she heeded this advice and preserved Asbury and his mamma. After the "Holy Ghost, emblazoned in ice instead of fire, continued, implacable, to descend" in the final scene of "The Enduring Chill," Flannery writes in her new manuscript, "Walter wrenched himself away and lurched out of bed. He ran from the room as if from a gathering of devils."[14] Now what?

In contrast to "The Enduring Chill," the Asbury in the sequel is not merely morbid but suicidal, trying, through volition alone, to end his life. He composes a final will and testament, converses with his sister (still called Mary George and not yet Mary Maud) about the best course for suicide, and even discusses death with his father, Tilman, who has not had a stroke, as he has in the rest of the *Why Do the Heathen Rage?* papers. This version of Walter's father is more innocent and childlike than the raging old man of the rest of the third-novel drafts. He brings his son a piece of chocolate pie and a carton of cigarettes as a peace offering before death. Although Asbury is named Walter in these scenes, he is a rendition of Asbury—an artist, a previous New York resident, morbid, sick, and on the verge of tears in each encounter. His prophesied death by kidney failure is the more disturbing, considering O'Connor herself died this way.

Chocolate Pie

Why Do the Heathen Rage?

WALTER'S LAST WILL
AND TESTAMENT[1]

Walter was creating his death. So, what? He tried to grasp the hugeness of it again, but it appeared distant, a matter of faith, not of knowledge. Something that he might forget himself if he did not write it down. After a moment, he got up unsteadily and made his way across the room to the large rolltop desk. In the first drawer, he found one ball-point pen that would write and what was left of an old Blue Horse note pad—a few lined pages attached to the back cardboard. He carried these back to the bed. With action came a kind of bitter inspiration. They respected whatever sounded legal. If he wrote it in the form of a will, they would be more likely to credit it with truth. And it would eat into them; if not at once, eventually.

For some time, he sat with his knees raised to support the pad and tried to think how he could say it. At the top of the sheet, he scratched LAST WILL AND TESTAMENT and then began, "I, Walter Grandstaff Tilman, being of sound mind, do hereby will and bequeath . . ." and stopped. Nothing more came. The two boulders in his head seemed to grind up each potential thought before he could grasp it. He had not been able to concentrate for the last two months, why should he think he could now. Presently, he wrote, "my death," and stopped again. They would say he was "temporarily not himself." Finally, with distaste, he put "to humanity." He disliked grandiose words like "humanity," but that was all he could think of. It was better than "mankind," which sounded religious. The thing was to say why. He let the pad rest on his stomach and with the blunt end of the pen he traced circles on the bed sheet. Drowsiness began to overcome him. Twice he jerked his head up as it was about to roll to the side. Finally, he closed his eyes for a moment. He awoke with a start.

His sister was standing by the side of his bed, one hand on her hip and the other holding the pad with the beginning of the will on it. She was reading it. He lurched up and tore it out of her hand.

"Whaddya want?" he said furiously. "Whaddya standing there with your nose in my business for?"

Around Mary George people reverted to their childhood. It was impossible to act any age around her but eleven. She was short and plump and had delicate pale skin and an upturned nose on which was perched a pair of pink-rimmed spectacles. Her hair drifted out from a pile on top of her head. She had small brown busy-body eyes and a Doctor of Education degree. Nothing would settle her, he thought, but a large, stupid, demanding man.

She continued to stand there, her arms folded. "So, what are you willing your death to humanity for?" she asked. "What's humanity supposed to do with it?" She could make the word "humanity" seem hilarious. The intensity of her gaze forced sudden words out of him.

"If man is divine," he said, "he can die at will. Just by deciding that he doesn't care for the farce. He can know what he's doing. He can prefer to die and do it."

"How come you don't just put your head in the oven?" she asked.

"Because that's what cowards do," he said. "This way the mind is in control. The mind does it. We're evolving toward this. In a couple of million years this is the way people'll die—just by deciding they've had enough. That's why I'm leaving my death to humanity, so they can learn."

"You're the first?"

"Yes."

"The trouble with you is you're too big for your britches and always have been," she said.

"The trouble with me," he said in a voice just on the verge of breaking, "is that I'm much too small for them. That's my whole point but I wouldn't expect you to understand anything like that. If there's a God, he's done nothing for me."

"There's no God," his sister said.

"Thanks for that information," he muttered. "I figured you would know."

Once when Mary George was thirteen and he was six, she had lured him with the promise of an unnamed present into a large tent full of people and had dragged him by the arm up to the front where a man in a blue suit and red and white tie was standing. "Here," she said in a loud voice, "I'm already saved but you can save him. He's a real stinker." He had broken her grip and shot out of there like a small cur and later, when he had asked for his present, she had said, "You would have got Salvation if you had waited for it, but since you acted the way you did, you get nothing!"

She shook her head and moved away toward the door where she paused and considered him again. "The State Hospital is not so bad anymore," she said. "They had a big stink about it in the papers and they've improved it a lot. You wouldn't have to stay long. A couple of shock treatments would fix you up."

"Mary George!" her mother hissed, coming up behind her with the dinner tray. "Don't talk like that. Go get the bed tray out of my closet. All you need is food and rest," she said, coming in, "and you'll be good as new."[2]

"I'm not hungry," he said. "I don't want that. You can just take it back."

She set the tray down temporarily on the seat of the chair. He looked at the steaming dinner with disgust—fresh pork, black-eyed peas, turnip greens, squash, sweet potatoes, four large biscuits and a giant glass of tea with a half inch of sugar in the bottom of it—the meal of a prosperous field hand.

"I'll bring your dessert later," she said.

"Hurry up, Sister," she called.

Mary George ambled back in unfolding the legs of a yellow bed tray. "Now sit back and let Sister put that across your lap," his mother said. Mary George slung the tray across his lap and his mother set the dinner tray down on it.

He could not trust himself to say anything, even to shout at them to go to hell, for fear he would burst into tears. His sister took the napkin and flipped it open and then had the effrontery to stick it in the neck of his pajamas.

"Now you eat every bit of that," his mother said. "Ours is getting cold downstairs." And they left him with it.

Tears of rage and frustration began to travel down his face. Nevertheless, he started eating the dinner and after the first forkful, he ate with a steady desperate concentration like a man who had not had a meal in a month. In New York he had eaten like a Negro—light bread and sardines; he had even sopped the bread in sardine oil to get all of it and he had gloried in this poverty. Even after he had realized that there was no hope of his being an artist, he had still, for a while, gloried in it. His sardine cans went into the garbage clean and dry; he used a tea bag four times. There was a girl from Kansas who lived on the floor under him whose mother sent her a box once a month. When she had a box, she brought it up and they had cleaned it out, and afterward they slept together. The girl was plain and though he had eaten her boxes ravenously he had always been glad to get back to the light bread and sardines and to know that she wouldn't come back again until she had the excuse of another box. Once he had come to the realization that he had no talent, his poverty appeared to be a good in itself, the only thing he had left that seemed to promise that it held something back, that it had some reserve of dignity to lend to a man who knew he was mediocre. Then that too gave way and he had nothing.

He looked around the room warily. Everything was mammoth and steady—the black antique highboy, the giant wardrobe, the old rolltop desk, each stood there like a Grandstaff ancestor who had taken this form for eternity. Each seemed to give him his choice: he could be wrong or he could be crazy. He could conform or he could stick to his wrongheadedness and go to the state hospital. And, each seemed perfectly sure of his choice, confident that he would take the safer and more comfortable course, confident that he was no martyr for a silly idea. His heavy forehead sank in his hands, and he knew it too. He knew that when the moment of decision came, he would make the small decision, the less generous one, the one with the least risk. If he had had a coat-of-arms, the motto on it would have been "Safety First." Generosity and imagination had not quite been bred out of him—he had just enough of both to make him miserable—but the courage to act on them had.

Creaking footsteps, Tilman's, sounded on the stairs. Walter hadn't actually looked at his father for several years or listened to him in longer than that. They had written each other off early as extremists. It was bitter to Tilman to have an only son who was no better than a Bolshevik—his term for anyone who left Presley County—and it had been disagreeable to Walter (though no more than he expected) to find that his father was a caricature, too grotesque to belong even in Southern fiction. He had tried once to put him in a story and his mere presence had turned it farce.

The old man reached the top step and paused for a moment in the door. His bright blue eyes divided his face evenly—the lower half ruddy and weather-hardened, the upper pale as death and rising through a patch of thick ethereal white hair to an elfin peak at the top. Without the brown shed of his hat brim shading his expression, Tilman looked old and childlike and without guile. He gazed for a moment solemnly at Walter. Walter's mouth went a little slack and his heart began to pound. If he had met the old man on the street, he might not have known him. Tilman had aged 20 years since he had seen him last. Tilman came in, his face respectful as if he might have been entering the Camp Creek Baptist Church of a Sunday with his hat in his hand. He carried a plate with a generous sized piece of chocolate pie on it; in his other hand, he carried a carton of cigarettes. The pie fork was in his shirt pocket.

He came creeping up to the bed and carefully laid the carton of cigarettes beside Walter's pillow.

"I bought you those there," Tilman said. Then he set the pie plate down in the greasy dinner plate and removed the fork from his shirt pocket and set it on top of the pie. His hands were an ancient red and shook noticeably. "The women sent you this here," he said. He stood for a moment, then he said, "Sick eh."

Walter swallowed. He nodded. He raised himself in the bed and fumbled appreciatively with the carton of cigarettes.

"Thanks," he mumbled.

"You might as well smoke," the old man said, "and have you all the little pleasures you can whilst you're here."

Walter nodded. "We don't come from long lived people," Tilman said. Walter began to eat the pie. Tilman stood there and watched.

"My daddy died when he was twenty-eight years of age," Tilman said in an elegiac voice. "We don't come from long lived people. My granddaddy lived to be thirty-two. I'm almost eighty-odd year, but I'm a sport. I'll live to be a hundred. We come of people that run to kidney failure. I would be dead now if I hadn't got rid of that rotten kidney. Is it your kidneys failing?"

Walter shook his head. "It's something general," he mumbled.

"You had two aunts died consumptive," Tilman said. "They were Wordsheds. The Grandstaffs run to heart attacks. The Wiggins have cancer. But the Tilmans run to kidney failure early in life. What color's your urine?" he asked.

"I don't know," Walter said. "It feels like my head's in a clamp," he said in a suffocated voice.

"That's kidney failure," Tilman said. "What did Block say about your urine?"

"He just got blood."

"Blood!" the old man exclaimed. "Every year I'd give you less for a doctor. You can't tell nothing from blood. You have your answers in your urine."

Walter laid his fork down on the pie.

"If it's only one kidney failed," Tilman said, "you might could have that out. Then you might live a few years longer."

"I don't want to live," Walter said in a choked voice.

Tilman stood there. The lower half of his face went through a little contortion. "The Tilmans run to kidney failure," he said.

Walter pushed the fork into the pie again.

Tilman looked around the room. "You don't have you a radio," he said. "I'll get you one if you want it."

Walter shook his head.

"I'll get you a television," Tilman said. "You might as well . . ."

Walter shook his head. "I don't want this pie," he whispered.

"Well I'll take the tray," Tilman said and tears began running down his cheeks. "And if it's anything you want, boy," he said in a high voice, "you call on me. Not the women. Me." He picked up the tray and shuffled off toward the door with it in an apparent hurry.

Walter lay there stunned. A welter of emotions fought in him: self-pity and a return of the wild ridiculous affection for his father that he had had only when he was six. What seemed to be a snake bedded in his stomach began slowly to wake and uncoil and his whole body shook with morbid laughter. He sat up and held his head in his hands. He staggered up and moved toward the bathroom. The sound of his retching was drowned out by a guinea that had flown onto the tin roof and paused there to send his raucous cry like static on the quiet noon air. He came out again in a little while with bloodshot eyes and made his way across a reeling room and fell in his bed again. He was too sick even to relish the thought that he was worsening, that none of this was illusion. By night fall, his fever was 104.

Tilman sat on the porch weeping, as was fitting, for an only son doomed to die before his father. The old man rocked steadily like a man with the reins of time in his hands. "The Tilmans run to kidney failure," he said. "He waddn't a bad boy. It's the world has run to seed. He never had a chance."

For Flannery O'Connor, death may have been more familiar and more pressing after she returned home to Milledgeville in 1950. When asked about her fascination with death in her stories, O'Connor responded, "I'm a born Catholic and death has always been brother to my imagination. I can't imagine a story that doesn't properly end in it or in its foreshadowings." Her ability to dramatize the reminder of death (*memento mori*) in her fiction sounds strange in a culture petrified by the fear of death. We postpone all thoughts of death by strenuous workout regimens, plastic surgery, overly full daily itineraries. O'Connor had no such luxury to quiet the reminder of death—she was in and out of the hospital for more than a decade, especially in the later years. All the while, she was working on this "longish piece of fiction that [she] hope[s] will turn out to be a novel," as she admits.[3]

Suicide would be an easy out for someone in such pain, and she writes about a man who contemplates that possibility. His desire to will his death with his mind is a parody of the Nietzschean will to power. It mocks the existentialist cartoon: we can imagine Walter donning a black turtleneck at this point and spending his leisure hours at a coffee shop in the Bronx reading Jean-Paul Sartre. His last will and testament is comical. In "The Enduring Chill," Asbury believes he has hastened home to die but decides that "suicide would not have been a victory."[4] He saves his mother the public embarrassment of a suicide and instead leaves a letter detailing his mother's failings, to be opened after he dies.

When Walter dedicates his death to abstract "humanity," we should note that O'Connor may have been reading Henri de Lubac's *The Drama of Atheist Humanism* at this time (she dated her copy 1963). In this book, the *ressourcement* theologian points out how atheist philosophers such as Ludwig Feuerbach, Friedrich Nietzsche, and Auguste Comte uplift a false vision of "humanity" in which human beings lack embodied souls; these writers do not dwell in the concrete experience of reality. De Lubac uses Dostoevsky's character Alexei Kirillov (from the novel *Demons*) as an example of someone who takes these ideas to the extreme by committing suicide, proof that he wills his existence, or, in this case, nonexistence. The word "humanity," it seems, had already become vogue among Walter's hip contemporaries and had none of the religious connotations of "mankind."

Walter's discussion with Mary George about the existence of God begins and ends quickly with the conclusion that there is no God. An earlier scene shows Asbury/Walter in New York dialoguing with a priest named Vogle about the existence of God, as well as about their domineering mothers (Vogle's mother being the Catholic Church). In "The Enduring Chill," Father Ignatius Vogle is undaunted by Asbury's heresy. The man appeals to Asbury as "a man of the world." In the unfinished *Why Do the Heathen Rage?* manuscripts, Asbury explains:

> All the creative energy has been drained out of me. You would have to know my mother. My sister. My father. . . . She's a manager.

Asbury sounds as though he's speaking to a counselor as he blames all of his inadequacies on his mother. Vogle responds with an attempt to draw Asbury from the personal to the spiritual:

> "I have a managing mother," said Vogle with his dry smile. "Holy Mother. Maybe our experiences have not been altogether different. I might have been an artist."
>
> They studied each other. Asbury leaned forward. "Do you believe in God?"
>
> Vogle smiled wearily. "I believe in my mother," he said.[5]

Although Vogle jokes about "Mother Church," his quip might be one Flannery herself could have made about her own mother, Regina. But the dialogue is reminiscent of a conversation from Dostoevsky's *The Idiot*: standing before the painting by Holbein of the dead Christ in his tomb, Rogozhin asks Prince Myshkin, "Do you believe in God?"

Just a few years after Flannery's death, *Time* magazine featured the question "Is God Dead?" on its 1966 cover. But, in these unfinished episodes dating to the early 1960s, the Tilmans already assume that God is dead. They are ahead of the theologians. O'Connor readers may hear an echo of the Bible salesman from "Good Country People," who exclaims, "I been believing in nothing ever since I was born!"[6]

How did O'Connor write about the realities that she believed in for readers who believed in nothing? The problem, as she describes it in her essays, is that for the modern audience "religious feeling has become, if not atrophied, at least vaporous and sentimental." She chooses to scandalize her readers, to dramatize belief as a "stumbling block" in the way of her characters. O'Connor structures her stories to lead toward a character's moment of grace, the moment where each may choose whether or not to believe in God, and O'Connor intends this God to be the "God of Abraham, Isaac and Jacob" as well as "the one who became man and rose from the dead."[7] As often as not, characters trip and fall over the question of this belief, but some of them rise back up. We tend to focus on the characters who stay down—or stay dead: the grandmother from "A Good Man Is Hard to Find," Mrs. May, Mrs. Shortley. But, following their revelations, the ending for some is left open, such as with Mrs. Turpin, O. E. Parker, Julian, and Asbury. In the majority of her work, O'Connor builds toward this epiphanic encounter as the climax of the story. However, O'Connor wanted to begin this unfinished novel with the conversion. Walter sometimes speaks of a "revolting conversion which he had neither been able to throw off or warm up."[8] In the conversation with his sister, Walter recalls a religious interaction from his childhood. He remembers fleeing a church revival. The following is another scene in the manuscripts, in which Walter is baptized at a summer camp by a reverend named Simcox who never appears in the story again. But, like the revival, the baptism reflects Walter's aversion to faith, finding conversion "revolting."

Ancestral Water

Why Do the Heathen Rage?

BAPTISM[1]

W alter and Mr. Simcox had fallen into each other's hands once when Walter was thirteen. Simcox had baptized him and had never seen him again. The baptism had taken place in the rock pool outside Camp Creek at noon one Sunday. Walter was fourth in a line of sheet-draped boys his age who had become convinced at camp that baptism was necessary for salvation. He had put rubber plugs in his ears. The other three went down nervously grinning and came up, each with a hideous little gasp, as if beneath the water there had been a vision of reality none was prepared for. The thought of bolting flashed at Walter just as Simcox grasped him and threw him backwards with vicious unexpected strength into the crystal-clear water where a thousand microcosmic suns bounced. Walter felt nothing but Simcox's unwanted hands gripping him by the arms.

Simcox does not get fleshed out much in the *Why Do the Heathen Rage?* episodes. He's a mere caricature of a country preacher. In a rough draft of the scene where Walter dialogues with Vogle in New York, Walter imitates "Brother Simcox," whom he calls "Tilman's preacher."

"Believe ye on the Lord Jesus Christ and ye shall be saved,"
Walter said in the nasal voice of Brother Simcox. The others
laughed. The priest did not. Walter's face grew red.[2]

Walter's joke echoes a similar either-or ultimatum from
O'Connor's 1955 story "The River." A country preacher named
Bevel Summers calls out, "Believe in Jesus or the devil!" be-
fore he baptizes Harry Ashfield. The same choice is set before
Francis Tarwater in *The Violent Bear It Away*, where baptism
also drives the action of the story.

Because her readers generally assume that "baptism is a
meaningless rite," O'Connor determined "to arrange the action so that this baptism carries enough awe and terror to jar
the reader into some kind of emotional recognition of its significance."[3] As a Catholic, Flannery O'Connor was baptized as
an infant. She lived across the street from the church where
she received this first rite, so her parents merely carried her
into the building as though visiting a neighbor. Ever since that
Easter Sunday on which she was baptized, the church would
have been as familiar to her as home.

Yet, in the South, the majority of believers are Protestants
who select baptism as a rite of passage into the congregation
once they reach the "age of reason." O'Connor admits to a
friend, "All voluntary baptisms are a miracle to me and stop
my mouth as much as if I had just seen Lazarus walk out of the
tomb."[4] She jokes that she wouldn't have found any reason for
baptism had she not received it as a child. The joke relies on the
understanding that such a practice appears unreasonable. Like
the other sacraments, baptism relies not on reason alone but on
faith in the authority of revelation, of biblical commandments,
and of church teaching.

When O'Connor's characters choose baptism, they are
children arguably not at the age of reason. Harry Ashfield is
four or five; the narrator is not sure. O'Connor defends this
young age to a producer who hoped to adapt "The River" into

an off-Broadway production: "The credibility of such a story depends on the age of the boy: a five year old child might reasonably be expected to believe that another world could be found under the river; a six year old one wouldn't."[5] While Walter struggles against Simcox as he's pushed beneath the water, Harry longs for baptism as an escape from his unhappy family life. When the preacher Bevel asks Harry if he wants "to go to the Kingdom of Christ" and "be washed in the river of suffering," Harry says yes because he assumes he "won't go back to the apartment then, I'll go under the river."[6] While the reasons an adult would choose submersion in the waters of baptism confounded O'Connor's imagination, she could understand that the sufferings of childhood would compel one to seek the kingdom of Christ. Instead of placing Walter's baptism at the climax of the story, O'Connor sets it in a flashback, one seemingly meaningless episode in his childhood.

O'Connor knew firsthand "that anybody who has survived his childhood has enough information about life to last him the rest of his days."[7] Although she probably did not intend to include more than a paragraph or two of flashback on Walter's childhood, she drafted scenes from his past, calling him Asbury. These scenes are like character sketches where O'Connor works out his background and what made Walter into the sour, disgruntled twenty-eight-year-old of her novel in progress. One can see how much his character altered from his genesis in Asbury to his creation as Walter.[8]

Unsung

Why Do the Heathen Rage?

WALTER/ASBURY'S CHILDHOOD[1]

B y the end of the summer Asbury's health had been restored sufficiently to permit him to wander idly about the place on horse-back. When he was growing up, he had developed a convenient allergy to horseflesh in order not to be sent for the cows. A similar affliction caused by chicken feathers had kept him away from the henhouse. And he had kept himself out of the 4H club by sheer will power, by hunching his shoulders and ducking his head and turning on his heel, full in the face of his mother's saying, "I'm ashamed of you, ashamed of you. How do you expect to ever run this place yourself if you don't learn how to do something? Look at Billie Watts!" Billie Watts was a fat sallow boy a little younger than Asbury who had had his picture in the paper standing solemnly beside a Duroc hog that he very much resembled. Watts, having fulfilled his early promise, was now pioneering with pig parlors, the first in the area.

Asbury's mother didn't know if she had got him started wrong or what. She pondered whether sometime during the age of three and five, he might have had some experience which had prejudiced his subconscious mind against nature. Mary George who was an expert on child psychology had selected a very elementary book on the subject and given it to her to read, and although she thought they were pretty far-fetched she toyed with various advanced theories. When he was two, he had been attacked by a goose who had raised four blood-blisters on his face and could very easily have put out his eye, but so far as she knew this was his only frightening encounter he had had with an animal. He had never liked ponies or guinea pigs, never caught snakes or frogs and even man's best friend did not interest him. Mrs. Fox felt that every boy should have a dog and consequently he had had a dog, but he paid it no attention and did not even name it. The dog, for his part, did not take any interest in Asbury either. They went their separate ways as if with a mutual aversion.

It was not only his attitude toward animals that caused his mother concern, there were other things. He did not like to go barefooted. It was well known to her that every normal boy rich or poor liked to go barefooted, but Asbury seemed to suffer some invisible nervous torment every time his bare skin touched the bare earth, as if he were allergic to the very ground he walked on. He was not excessively fastidious, he had no feminine qualities, he was always ready to fight, and he early developed a brand of sass that seemed to cover more than the situation at hand. She sensed in it a sneer, directed around and behind her, that eluded her and yet hung in the air. Sometimes she took several hours discovering the real offensiveness of one of his remarks.

He had always seemed to have an excessive self-concern, even as a small boy. When told or asked to do something he had had the habit of pausing, his blue eyes fixed suspiciously as if he were consulting himself as to his own best interests before he moved. This introspection did not produce a dreamy state. He seemed always intensely aware of where he was, as if he were trying to scent some hostile force in the air that might any second take shape and threaten him.

Flannery O'Connor creates about a dozen children running through her complete stories, nearly all of them annoying: John Wesley and June Star ("A Good Man Is Hard to Find"); the despairing, tragic case of Bevel/Harry Ashfield ("The River") and poor, neglected Norton ("The Lame Shall Enter First"); the obstinate but righteously just Mary Fortune Pitts ("A View from the Woods"); the unnamed wannabe martyr in "The Temple of the Holy Ghost"; the unnamed pest of "A Circle in the Fire." O'Connor was not partial to the idea of writing children as miniature saints. "Stories of pious children tend to be false," she claims in the introduction to *A Memoir of Mary Ann*. "I never cared to read about little boys who build altars and play they are priests, or about little girls who dress up as nuns, or about those pious Protestant children who lack this equipment but brighten the corners wherever they are."[2] Yet most of her child characters, if not innocent, are victims who die at the hands of sinful adults. Asbury's childhood aversion to the animal kingdom indicates he will be neither an innocent nor a tragic figure, but more like a villain—a heathen. Perhaps his villainous inclinations will be redeemable. When O'Connor writes about Walter's childhood, she builds off Asbury's earlier repugnance for animals and increases in this character an affinity for sin.

Why Do the Heathen Rage?

WALTER RECITES
THE TEN COMMANDMENTS[1]

C hildren have an instinct for keeping themselves free. One of
Tilman's desires was to see his son's picture in the 4H news
alongside a prize Duroc hog, the faces of boy and hog shining with
health and satisfaction and plain country virtues. But Walter's face
did not shine. His attention appeared withdrawn to some interior
problem: had there been any shine about him, it would have been the
light catching on his glasses. The hogs he raised under duress looked
unhappy and thin and never made the local paper. Once he poisoned
one of them and the shock changed his life.

The sow had almost been ready to farrow and the idea that he could
prevent this came to him quite casually as he lay in bed. He sat upright
in the dark astonished. He was thirteen at the time, and he had never
poisoned anything before. He had never thought of it. He was not
a child who lacked prudence and he had inherited a respect for the
law. Rapidly he went through the Ten Commandments in his mind.
Thou shalt love the Lord thy God with thy whole heart and thy whole
soul and thy whole mind and thou shalt not put graven images before
him. Thou shalt love thy neighbor as thyself. Thou shalt not take the
name of the Lord in vain. Remember to keep Holy the Sabbath Day.
Thou shalt honor thy father and thy mother. Thou shalt not kill. But
this meant people. They killed hogs every fall. It could not mean what

you ate. Thou shalt not bear false witness against thy neighbor. Thou shalt not steal. Thou shalt not commit adultery. He did not know what adultery was but he thought that if it had been about hogs, he would have known. Thou shalt not covet thy neighbor's wife. Thou shalt not covet thy neighbor's goods. Nowhere was there anything about poisoning hogs, especially your own hogs. He lay down and thought of the more remote prospect of his being prosecuted civilly.

O'Connor's dilemma is how "to make corruption believable" so that the reader understands the significance of grace.[2] Unlike in ages past, twentieth-century readers and beyond assume ontological goodness—worse than that, many assume they are divine, gods unto themselves. In *Bad Religion*, Ross Douthat writes about this fallacy common among readers.[3] He uses Elizabeth Gilbert, the author of *Eat, Pray, Love*, as a prime example; she encourages readers to recognize that "somewhere within us all, there does exist a supreme self who is eternally at peace. That supreme Self is our true identity, universal and divine." Our life objective is to "honor the divinity that resides within [us]," Gilbert suggests.[4] Although Gilbert published decades after O'Connor, she merely makes explicit what O'Connor's readers had assumed for years. Mrs. May from "Greenleaf" exemplifies this reader; she is "a good Christian woman with a large respect for religion, though she did not, of course, believe any of it was true."[5] For Mrs. May, there is no god higher than herself. Right before her comeuppance, she imagines standing before the Almighty's throne and being able to show him how hard she worked, daring him to find anything wrong with her. How to convince such readers of what O'Connor believed—that they need a divine Savior outside themselves?

In each of O'Connor's stories, she broaches this impasse with varying means. In "The Lame Shall Enter First," a schoolteacher plays savior to the social deviant but needs grace himself; in "The Displaced Person," a woman farmer hires a displaced person not out of kindness but for mercenary ends, only to dehumanize and dispose of him. As O'Connor explains in her essays, "The business of fiction is to embody mystery through manners"[6]—the manners change but not the mystery.

For her third novel, O'Connor set her attention on the problem of love and relationships between white and Black characters. In a letter, she confesses why this predicament became the focus for her final work: "I feel very good about those changes in the South that have been long overdue—the whole racial picture. . . . All this affects my writing by keeping me at it. It's great fuel for my kind of comedy and my kind of tragedy."[7] If only we could ask O'Connor: In this final novel, what was to be the comedy and what the tragedy? Or, rather, who was the heathen? Who the saint?

I imagine Flannery and her mother early in the morning in their small kitchen, sharing the thermos of coffee that had been brewed the night prior. The radio would be on with the morning news, and outside a few wake-up calls from competing roosters and peacocks interrupt the darkness.

Although Flannery insisted that Regina never read any of her stories, we can hope they discussed her works in progress, as writers often do. Regina knew about the working title, *Why Do the Heathen Rage?* She was concerned because it was the same title as an Atlanta businessman's regular newspaper column.

"That man is going to sue us for stealing his title," Regina apparently worried.

"It's from the Bible. Only one liable to sue is God," Flannery might have retorted.

The column "Why Do the Heathen Rage?" ran in sixty newspapers nationwide. An anonymous author vehemently denounces the immorality of American leaders, the waywardness of our youth, and the failings of the church. Littered with exclamation marks—like Oona's letters—the columns preached the wrath of God, making the author sound like a twentieth-century Jonathan Edwards.

The King James Version of the Bible uses the phrase "Why do the heathen rage?" twice, once in the Old Testament and once in the New Testament. O'Connor had a Catholic study Bible, the Douay-Rheims Version, that she marked up. In their biblical context, the words are first attributed to King David of Israel, who questions why people, especially those in powerful positions, scheme in vain against God and his people (Psalm 2:1). The question is repeated in the New Testament as a group of converts celebrates the release of the apostles Peter and John from the threats of the Jewish Sanhedrin (Acts 4:25).

There are many ties between O'Connor's work in progress and these two sources for her title. The column could have been written by a converted Walter later in his life—a secular contemplative transformed into a vigilant man of God who uses his pen to express his condemnation of society's evils. Peter and John are apostolic versions of the worldly Oona. In the account in Acts, after reciting this psalm, the people relinquish all their possessions, much as Oona's Friendship, Inc., does. Yet they do so not from their desire to follow Jesus but from their contempt for money.[8]

In November 1962, O'Connor wrote to her editor Robert Giroux, "Right now I am writing something that may prove longer than I'd like. It's tentatively called 'Why Do the Heathen Rage?' It's been inevitable I get around to that title sooner or later."[9]

In my imagination, Regina turns off the radio. She begins to pin her hat in place as the two women prepare to attend Mass. With a bobby pin between her teeth, she asks Flannery, "Which one is the heathen?"

"Both," Flannery answers, as she hobbles out of the kitchen on her crutches.

That's how I read the story: both Walter and Oona are the heathen. As are we all.

EPISTOLARY BLACKFACE

Limited by lupus, O'Connor traveled as much as she dared, but her health prevented her from seeing friends who lived at a distance as often as she may have liked. Much of her socializing was through her daily correspondence. She answered as many letters from strangers as from friends. One of her closest friends, Betty Hester, was introduced to her via mail. People whom she would have had little patience to endure in person received at least a terse response by letter. The problem with friendship through the mail is the ability to mask yourself from the other person, to hide your face or edit your immediate response to what they wrote. You can craft your output to exhibit yourself through letters however you'd like to appear. O'Connor seems to have played this game with Maryat Lee, putting on the caricature of a racist, uneducated Southerner in her responses to her friend. They signed their letters with pseudonyms drawn from O'Connor's stories. Maryat would sign "Asbury" and O'Connor, "Tarwater."

In *Why Do the Heathen Rage?* Walter has the opportunity to become other people through letters. Like a chameleon, he becomes whatever his correspondent wants to see. He compliments the poor poetry of a woman who sends him a verse each day; he confesses false doubts to a Methodist minister. Then he pretends to be Black to test the affections of Oona Gibbs, a woman who desperately desires to love all people, even though she herself does not like the word "love" and does not know what it means. He reflects on his game:

He had more friends he had never seen than friends he had met.
The soul moves quickly without the body. Flesh is the greatest
interference to love.[1]

He defines "love" as "ethereal." Like Mr. Shiftlet from "The
Life You Save May Be Your Own," Walter divides the body
from the soul. Mr. Shiftlet explains to the old woman, "A man
is divided into two parts, body and spirit. . . . The body, lady,
is like a house: it don't go anywhere; but the spirit, lady, is like
a automobile: always on the move, always." Walter copies this
other twenty-eight-year-old character in their shared modern
Gnosticism. Both of them deflect any reminders that the soul
affects the body and vice versa.

Yet Walter's theory about the disconnect between body and
soul is tested when he tries to perceive life through the eyes of
a Black man. When Walter attempts to expose what he believes
is Oona's false love for the oppressed with his own charade,
he emphasizes the reality of the concrete world more than he
desires to admit. The narrator observes of Walter,

> As far as Negroes went, his fictional sense was inadequate. He
> could only look at them from the outside. Who knew Eustis'
> thoughts or Roosevelt's or Alice's?[2]

Walter is choosing to mask his white face with what can only
be a cartoon of a Black persona and is not realizing how far he
fails to relate with whom he believes is Other.

For twenty-first-century readers, Walter's ruse may appear to
come out of nowhere. Yet it was likely inspired by John Howard
Griffin, the white journalist who, in 1959, darkened his skin to
pass as a Black man and ventured south of the Mason-Dixon line
to uncover firsthand the "plight of the Negro." Flannery had at
least two opportunities to visit with the author of *Black Like Me*.
Her friend Father McCown was an activist who knew Griffin. She
writes, "If John Howard Griffin gets to Georgia again, we would
be delighted to see him; but not in blackface. I don't in the least

blame any of the people who cringed when Griffin sat down beside them. He must have been a pretty horrible-looking object."[3] The spectacle was still on her mind in May 1964 when she recalls that her friend Billy Sessions ran into Griffin "in his blackface" at a monastery and was set to bring him to visit Milledgeville. O'Connor says she found the simulation too disturbing. She writes, "I don't mean hysterical ha ha but hystericaleek."[4]

Around the same time that O'Connor is incorporating this idea into her burgeoning novel, fellow Southern novelist Walker Percy is creating his pseudo-Black character in *The Last Gentleman*, another parody on Griffin. As Percy's pseudo-Black man explains, "The idea had come to him in the middle of the night: why not *be* a Negro?"[5] We hear Oona Gibbs say something similar in her letter to Walter: "I would like to come South and live with a Negro family—work, eat, sleep with them, share their burdens for a while. I would like to somehow *become* them."[6] Percy and O'Connor depict this posturing as preposterous and condescending.

O'Connor herself admits that she struggled with the idea of writing from the Black perspective, a concern she projects through Walter. When O'Connor depicted Black characters, she drew from the African Americans she knew, such as Louise and Jack Hill or Willie "Shot" Mason, who worked on her mother's farm. "I don't understand them [Black people] the way I do white people," she once confessed to an interviewer. "I don't feel capable of entering the mind of a Negro. In my stories they're seen from the outside."[7] Was this better than trying to assume an unfamiliar interior life or was this missing the common humanness of her characters? Decades later, the question about whether white writers can write Black characters has not been answered.

In 2016 Pulitzer Prize–winning poet Tyehimba Jess published *Olio*, a collection of poetry that defies labels, drawing the personas from African American performers before and after the Civil War. The book is described on its back cover as "an effort to understand how they met, resisted, complicated, co-opted, and sometimes defeated attempts to minstrelize them." For instance, in "Mark Twain v. Blind Tom," Jess aligns a factual quotation from Mark Twain about his encounter with "Blind Tom," a savant slave who was used to make money for his master by playing piano around the country, with Jess's fictional creation of Blind Tom's thoughts. In defiance of Twain's summation of Tom as a "dull clod" who does not comprehend more than a "stupid worm," Jess gives voice to the piano player: "I play the wind in my blood" and "I'm sent from above."[8] Of his own work, Jess says that he desires to deconstruct history and reconstruct it in a way "that helps us better understand it."[9] Seen only from outside themselves, the Black performers of the late nineteenth and early twentieth centuries were parodied and thus silenced. Through Jess's poetry, the voiceless receive a say.

One persona through whom Jess speaks is the blackface character from John Berryman's *Dream Songs*. Although Berryman writes through the voice of a "white American in early middle age," this character is "sometimes in blackface," which should have been as offensive then as it is now. Jess recasts the debatable dream songs as "freedom songs," insisting that for "those left behind . . . Berryman can't talk for them, can't tell my tale at all."[10] Similar to what O'Connor was attempting in Walter—a white man pretending to be Black—Berryman, in verse, has a white character put on blackface. Although critics have argued generous motives for Berryman, these authorial attempts to masquerade as Black characters often reduce Black identity to a caricature.[11]

Only a half dozen years before Berryman, O'Connor was navigating the tension involved in entering the inscape of her Black characters while recognizing her own limitations to understand a perspective seemingly foreign to her own. When I shared these passages with a friend who is a preacher at an African Methodist

Episcopal church, he lamented that O'Connor would feel distant from her Black characters at all, since we all share a similar humanity. It reminded me of Dorothy L. Sayers, who wrote her mystery novels from the perspective of Lord Peter Wimsey. "A man once asked me," Sayers writes, "how I managed in my books to write such conversation between men when they were by themselves?" Sayers answers, "I had coped with this difficult problem by making men talk, as far as possible, like ordinary human beings."[12] From Sayers's perspective, men and women share enough common humanity that she can depict men even without being one herself. However, a century before Sayers, Jane Austen purportedly would not write a scene with two men in dialogue because she had never been a man alone in a room with another man. She wrote of what she knew from her experience. Likewise, there are critics who accuse white writers of being unable to comprehend the Black perspective. When O'Connor fails to render Black characters except from outside them, she adopts the Austen caution rather than the audacity of Sayers.

Journalist Hilton Als credits O'Connor with prudence regarding her portrayal of Black characters in her work. While Als praises "the originality and honesty of her portrayal of Southern whiteness" and the realism rather than romanticism of her Black characters, he admits "she was sometimes clumsy at conveying real life among blacks beyond her own circles, . . . their communication with one another apart from whites." In her story "The Displaced Person," for instance, O'Connor writes dialogue between two Black characters that rings false, more like a rural "Amos 'n' Andy routine." From Als's perspective, it was better that O'Connor "rarely tried to cover this ground."[13] O'Connor may not have been able to render Black characters well from the inside out, but at least she knew the limits of her talent—she respected her characters enough not to regularly try.

In July 1964, as President Lyndon Johnson was signing the Civil Rights Act, O'Connor was on her deathbed. The world she knew and portrayed in her fiction was marked by a thick color line. O'Connor started writing *Why Do the Heathen Rage?* having never heard of "white supremacy." She knew nothing of "white privilege" or "fragility," Africanist presence, or even the 1980s fad with "color blindness." More than six decades have passed since O'Connor died, but—as Clint Smith reminds us in *How the Word Is Passed*—"In the long arc of the universe, even the most explicit manifestations of racism happened a short time ago."[14] While O'Connor mocks racism as ignorant, she unfortunately did not denounce it as evil. In her rigidly segregated world, O'Connor was relatively blind to the "explicit manifestations" that Smith documents.

For instance, in the 1960s, the N-word was an obscene word, but it did not, within O'Connor's white circles, connote violence, suffering, and death. From her privileged place in society, O'Connor knew less than she should have about the malicious deeds connected with the dehumanizing word, such as the hundreds of lynchings and assaults occurring in her home state. She intentionally places the racial slur in the mouths of her older characters, from whom she was accustomed to hearing it: the generation before Walter and Oona's, which includes Mr. and Mrs. Tilman, as well as Custer Boatright, a racist neighbor of the family. Although O'Connor appears to be unaware of the connection between this derogatory language and the horrific acts of assault, rape, and murder committed against African Americans, we in the twenty-first century are not. So, as we try to overcome centuries of pain caused by racism and as we are still seeing unjust violence against African Americans, how do we justify publishing a 1963 story written by a white Southern woman that employs the N-word?

In 2011 a small press in Alabama released a censored version of Mark Twain's *The Adventures of Huckleberry Finn*: all 219 uses of the N-word had been replaced with "slave."[15] Academics clamored to voice their opinions. An African American professor from Baylor University denounced the decision as a mistake that erases "the historical accuracy of the novel" and that "robs students" of a valuable learning experience.[16] Whether or not Twain's novel is racist, anti-racist, or both, what to do with the offensive language? For the N-word alone, the book was being censored, regardless of its content.

Linguist John McWhorter documents the fraught history of the N-word and its uses, as well as its recent transition from being considered improper to being considered shocking and egregious.[17] Although McWhorter mentions the move from Margaret Mitchell's employment of the word without reservation in the book *Gone with the Wind* (1936) to the film adaptation (1939), which refused to say the word at all, considering such slurs impolite at the least, he does not highlight the fact that Hollywood would have been more sensitive to such demeaning language than the South, where the language was used thoughtlessly by many white people. Only within the past twenty years has the word been banned from public speech. (There was even a 2002 book with the N-word as its title, documenting a history of the word.)[18]

In 2013 Oprah Winfrey stepped forward with a zero-tolerance policy for the N-word. *USA Today* ran Oprah's quote as the headline: "'You Cannot Be My Friend' and Use the N-word." The reason for her denunciation in the twenty-first century is obvious. "I always think of the millions of people," Oprah says, "who heard that as their last word as they were hanging from a tree."[19] In 2007 the mayor of Detroit oversaw a funeral for the word, organized by the NAACP: "Good riddance," Kwame Kilpatrick said. "Die, N-word." In response to these erasures, Ta-Nehisi Coates voiced a counterargument. Fully acknowledging the connotations of violence and cruelty associated with the N-word, Coates wrote, "But though we were born in violence, we did not

die there. That such a seemingly hateful word should return as
a marker of nationhood and community confounds our very
notions of power."[20] For Coates, the fact that white people are
barred from using the N-word shows how power shifts have
occurred in culture.

What then should we do about the N-word in *Why Do the
Heathen Rage?* If we're going to read these episodes not as historical archives but as literature, I'd recommend we attend to
what O'Connor suggests about characters who use the word.
We should think not only historically, about what the use of the
word communicates regarding the division between races, but
more theologically, about what the use of the word shows us
about how language can perpetuate hate instead of love. The
words we speak are acts of care or violence. In these unfinished
pages, characters speak offensively, and I hope we cringe to see
the N-word on the page (even the elided version, as we have
chosen to present it) and refuse to read it aloud. Yet, rather
than judge these characters haughtily—"oh, that we've come
so far!"—we should register the short distance between us and
them.

Reading O'Connor's 1960s unfinished novel, we must place
ourselves in her time rather than judge her by the standards
of our own. If every era suffers from cultural blindness, we
cannot assume we are without deficiencies as well. That admission does not excuse O'Connor for the way her fiction fails
to reach our knowledge of justice, but it gives us the humility
to appreciate the good in her stories. In Alan Jacobs's *Breaking Bread with the Dead*, he advises that we neither shrug our
shoulders at past writers' defects nor discard writers because
of their cultural assumptions. For instance, writing of Thomas
Jefferson and John Milton, Jacobs argues that we should admire those men for how they "pushed the world a little closer
to freedom and justice"[21] despite their human shortcomings
and temporal blindness. When we read O'Connor's work,

saturated as it is by her cultural moment, we seek the universal goods. In humility, we identify ourselves with O'Connor's characters, as what we are or could be if we fail to bridle our tongues, if we fail to name others as friends, and if we fail to care about the reality of the past and the truth about the present.

Letterhead

Why Do the Heathen Rage?

THE BLACK DOUBLE[1]

Three months ago, Walter had read in a small radical paper he received from New York an article by Oona Gibbs about Friendship, Inc. At once he had visualized her: a large woman with a blond pony-tail and a round childish face like Mary Maud's—the elementary school teacher on a larger, revolutionary scale, the world her first grade. Oona was a member of Friendship, Inc. This was a group of young people whose aim was to offer friendship wherever it was needed—to anyone at any place at any time. The members were pacifists, but they threw themselves with fervor into any fight where social injustice thrived. They championed Mexican migrant workers and Indians and Negroes and prisoners in general. Wherever there was social disturbance, they appeared on the spot to bear witness and taunt the police, and if possible, bring it to a head, though bearing witness was their main function. They wanted to suffer *with* the oppressed but not silently. Oona Gibbs would wear sandals and a peasant skirt and be a veteran of Mississippi jails.

He could visualize the lot of them, the whole pack of lean, hungry-eyed young people, moving from place to place on the scent of injustice. The very thought of them generated a peculiar fury in him, even though, as far as the moral issues were concerned, he was more or less on their side. Their naïveté and self-righteousness, their yearning for martyrdom stirred in him a rage equal to his father's. The article was poorly written. Hysteria affects syntax. Walter had sat down and written the woman a letter.

Ever since he was ten, Walter had been writing to people he did not know. Before he was fourteen, he had written to the President, his congressmen, authors, artists, people in the news. Notable people everywhere had heard from Walter and knew what he thought of them. His method then had been honest insult: "You stink" or worse. As he grew older, his interest in prominent people ceased. The relatively obscure began to hear from him. Sometimes he assumed personalities that fit the interests of his correspondents but most of the time he wrote legitimate letters to people he considered to have integrity. He had more friends he had never seen than friends he had met. The soul moves quickly without the body. Flesh is the greatest interference to love.

Only occasionally now did the urge come over Walter to write to somebody like Oona Gibbs whom he considered a fool. For three months, he had written to a woman poet whose ratty verse he could not abide letters of such overwhelming praise that she began sending him a poem each day, for she wrote one every night before going to bed. This was too much even for Walter. He wrote DECEASED across one of her letters and dropped it unopened back in the mail. Another time, he had had a correspondence with a Methodist minister who wrote a column in a church magazine his mother received. To him, he confessed himself torn by doubts which he detailed in imbecilic particularity. The minister faithfully reported these in his column with the correct solutions. Whenever one of his correspondents, from being a caricature, turned into a human being, pathetic, undemanding, full of ridiculous encroaching love, Walter wrote DECEASED across the letter he had just received and put it back in the mail, and for a time, like a child who has experienced shame, he would feel no more urge to debase himself again. He had a horror of the love of stupid people, or worse, of those who, not entirely stupid, nevertheless entertained the wrong ideas.

The time was long past that he should have written DECEASED across one of Oona Gibbs' letters, but he had not been able to bring himself to do it. Ever since the first letter, he had been held fast in the snares of his own depravity.

Every morning Walter walked to the highway to get the mail. The mailbox was a quarter of a mile from the house, down a red dirt road that ran between an old pecan grove on one side and the meadow with the four oaks in it on the other. A week after he had written her, he took out of the box his first letter from Oona Gibbs. It was in a plain cheap envelope and the address was typewritten. He held it tentatively to his nose. The letters of most of his correspondents had a distinctive odor. This one smelled like cheap paper with a faint undersmell of tobacco—the odor of the woman of the future. He opened it and saw that it was typewritten on yellow second sheets—an affectation of would-be literary people. The typing had a rushed spontaneous look, with many crossed out places as in letters of old friends. It began, "Dear Walter Tilman!" Nothing turned Walter's stomach faster than an exclamation point.

He put the letter back in the envelope, seeing he would need to sit down to read it. Midway up the road there was a huge rock in a ditch on the pecan grove side, on which he often sat to read his mail. He walked back up the road and settled himself on this—it was pleasantly warm beneath him, though the day was chilly—and removed the letter from the envelope. He began to read with a wry expression. His face grew brighter pink as he went along.

"What a joy to meet you," it began, "to receive such a warm generous letter, so full of real feeling for everything that matters. You want to know more about ourselves? All right! It's so simple as to be unbelievable.

"There are six of us so far—all of people whom lightning has struck. How? Who can say? Who cares? I was minding my own business when it happened to me and that is the great sin, that is the ONLY sin. Nothing else is sin. Believe me. Before it happened, I would never have done what you have done—voluntarily, open-heartedly, graciously written to ask about a movement that I would have considered absurd. But now I know that it is not absurd. It's life itself. I've become free.

"I've broken through the ceiling of everything that suffocated me—conventions, manners, religion—and have suddenly like breaking into outer space, understood that nothing matters but that you be open to everything and everybody. For the first time in my life, I'm afraid of nothing.

"To understand the change in me, you ought to know that one year ago I was Miss Conformity herself. I rushed to work every morning, worked all day at a fashion magazine, rushed back to a room at night to get ready for a date with one jackass or another, and at the end of the week, collected a check that had already been spent.

"That was me! I didn't even know who I was. But something was set to stop me. Something did. On my way to work, I passed an alley where there was a row of garbage cans, and every morning I glanced into it, and every morning I saw a Puerto Rican child standing there. He was waiting for the garbage. He had a paper bag. I guess he took it home. I looked at that child every day for three months before I saw him. Then one day I saw him. I didn't stop, but I saw him, and in the middle of the night I saw him again. I mean I SAW him, SAW him. I can't write. You have to use your imagination. You have the heart to know what happened to me. I saw him and then I saw myself and that was it.

"And this is the thing. I didn't want to give him food. I wanted to give him love. I wanted to stand with him. I wanted to say, 'Look, there are two of us here. We'll both get garbage.' Do you see? Yes, you see. You wrote me that wonderful letter and you see! The next morning I got up early, and I was going to talk to him but when he saw I was stopping, coming toward him, he ran. It was all I deserved.

"Six of us live in a flat on 2nd Avenue. None of us works. Food and rent come somehow. People take care of us. We give them a chance to show their love for us and we go show it for other people. Friendship is a weak word for this. We can't use the word 'love' because people take it the wrong way. Charity won't do because it sounds religious, and we aren't. There's none of that kind of nonsense about this. It's all in us! In you and me! It's something we've got and the prize is right now. The salvation is right now. There's no eternal reward, no postponement. You rot when you die and you only live once and then you only live when you love. Enuf for now."

Here, Walter turned his head to the side and his mouth pursed as if he had bitten into a sour orange—"Write me again! I want to know you. Tell me about the South. I weep for the poor black people of the South and for the white also because they are so blind. I would like to come South and live with a Negro family—work, eat, sleep with them, share their burdens for a while. I would like to somehow *become* them. How does a white Southerner stand it? Tell me! You have introduced yourself to me, made contact with another human being—HUMAN BEING, Walter Tilman! Love. The only word. Love from your old, new and always friend, Oona Gibbs."

Walter pulled his handkerchief from his back pocket and blew his nose vigorously. A huge shudder passed over him, which ended with a small, insidious, sensual tremor. He put the handkerchief back and returned the letter gingerly to the envelope. Then he sat holding it by the far corner as if it were something contaminated which must nevertheless be preserved.

"Good God in hell," Walter murmured.

His repulsion was deep and central. He felt a certain pull toward the letter and withdrew it again from the envelope. Skipping the words, he counted the exclamation points. Seventeen. His injured eye fell on the word "enuf." What enraged him was not this but something basic, something that offended the order of the universe. She admitted being someone whom lightning had struck. Lightning does not originate in the person.

He put the letter back in the envelope again and then sat there, gazing out across the meadow in the direction of the four oaks. The sky above them was dappled with small evenly shaped clouds as if giant feather pillows had been opened and their contents set drifting. Probably the girl was twenty-two or three, small, foolish, generous, and sooner or later to be a victim of her own good intentions. He saw a girl with very large, dark eyes and experienced a moment of tenderness for this image. Then it changed and he was faced with the big blond pony-tailed avenger. The woman had abrogated the place of God and set herself up where it had been. Her error was theological. The truth of this nourished him for almost a minute before he realized exactly what he was countenancing. He winced at the ease with which such a solution had come to him and to get it out of his mind, he began to plan a return letter to the woman.

He rose and started up the road, walking rapidly. Real inspiration did not come to him until he was almost in front of the house and saw the back of Roosevelt's head like a black globe resting on the balustrade.

That night Walter answered the woman's letter at galloping speed, throwing himself with such gusto into the role he was creating that when he finished, he saw before him a whole history for the character he had created. "Dear Miss Oona Gibbs," he wrote, "I have read your letter with a beating heart. I only expected information from you. I didn't really expect friendship, and I don't expect it now because as much as I want to believe in it, I don't believe you can give that friendship to me, and I'll tell you why. I will tell you, and if I never hear from you again, Miss Gibbs, I'll understand completely. Miss Gibbs, I am a Negro!" He considered putting several exclamation points here, but instead put only one.

"You may say that you would like to live and work with a Negro family, but I am afraid you don't know what you are talking about— with all respect to you, I say definitely, you don't know what you are talking about. I live with a Negro family on the place where I work, and I almost can't stand it myself. I work in the country for a white family, typical in every way of these parts. I nurse the old man. He had a stroke a few years ago. He can't walk, can't control himself, his mind is sometimes foggy, and his disposition is always terrible. He has a wife, a son 28 years old, who is an interesting slob-like character, and a school-teacher daughter a few years older, very bossy and self-important. I went to one of the state colleges for colored people for three years, and I am working to save up money to finish. My father—brace yourself Miss Gibbs—is in the chain-gang for slitting my mother's throat. If I ever slit anybody's throat, it will be my own.

"You may wonder how I am writing on a typewriter. Well, the son is in town now, the old lady is out in the field bossing the other Negro, and the old man is asleep for his afternoon nap. So, I am in the son's room, using his machine, hunt and peck more or less. In a way the son interests me, slob though he is. I don't think he would say anything if he knew I was using his typewriter. He wouldn't like it, but he couldn't say anything. His generation isn't sure which end is up. They can't order a Negro around; he can't even say 'n——' like his old man. What I mean is, he's eaten up with guilt on account of me; his old man never felt an ounce of it in his life. The son doesn't do any real work except he tends a liquor store for a few hours every night. The rest of the time he reads or writes or just ambles around, watching the way the light falls—like an old man looking at everything a lot before he dies. One thing I give him credit for, he's not going to get in the rat race, and I wish I had as much sense.

"I have enough sense to know that your friendship is not for me or my likes, Miss Gibbs, that it is much too innocent, that you are either a young lady fresh out of a fashionable college, or else a woman disappointed in life who has taken to arranging reality for other people. I don't know which and why should I care? I do care really, but I know enough to stay in my place and share this vast loneliness with no one. Yours sincerely, Walter Tilman."

It struck him as a very good letter.

"This vast loneliness" was just pretentious enough to strike her as profound. The pathetic corniness of the whole thing was just right, exactly what he imagined a poorly educated, intelligent, young Negro might write.

When the answer came, Walter removed it eagerly out of the box, held it an instant to his nose, recognized the scent, and took it smiling to the rock and opened it. His heart beat slightly more rapidly than usual. "Dear Walter Tilman, What a sniveling lump of self-pity you must be," he read. He looked up with an unpleasant expression and shifted his position on the rock. Then he continued to read. "It's quite likely that I could not stomach you, for I have learned one thing in the last year—only equals can be friends, and you don't appear to be my equal and not because you're black. Black and white is just a detail, like fat and thin, as far as I'm concerned."

"A rather significant detail," Walter muttered.

"For your information, I am not a woman disappointed in life. I have no desire to arrange reality for other people, though sometimes I would like to ask them why they don't arrange it for themselves. You, I doubt if you even vote. Are you registered? If you are, have you made any effort to see that other Negroes in your community register? You sound to me just like the type who complains and complains and never makes a move to do anything."

She'll be down here before long, registering Negroes, Walter thought.

"I suppose you spend a lot of time envying that stupid son on the place there where you work, wishing you were him. You sound like his double to me, only black, and without the place to do nothing on."

Walter's mouth pursed.

"Further for your information, I am not fresh out of a fashionable college. I never went to college. I went to work. And I don't think I have all the answers. I just think I'm on the right track. Maybe that letter I wrote you sounded over-excited and silly and maybe it was. It was just that nobody ever wrote me before and asked about what I thought or what I was doing. It went to my head, I guess. Or my heart. I don't always know what I'm doing. I follow a kind of scent like, all I've got is this sense that someday it'll lead me to the right place and to the right thing, that's all."

It's going to lead you into trouble, sister, Walter said to himself. She plunked down the word "black" as if she were throwing it in his face. The black double of the stupid son. He would have to give her credit for elementary intelligence. He should not have pretended to be such a lame-brained Negro. As far as Negroes went, his fictional sense was inadequate. He could only look at them from the outside. Who knew Eustis' thoughts or Roosevelt's or Alice's? But an educated

Negro, even a half-educated one, should be different. They were the ones who suffered. He should be able to get into such a mind. She had that radical kind of innocence that trails bloodshed behind it. He saw a small girl with grey intelligent eyes, glaring at him from beneath delicate black brows. He looked into the eyes coldly, but found himself drawn.

The thought of Oona Gibbs living with the Negroes on this place was comical. Walter would have liked to import her for one Saturday night of it. He thought the opportunity of observing a woman like Miss Gibbs was an exceptional one. He wondered what she looked like, and what suffocating conventions she flouted and what she had escaped into from her cramping religion besides openness to everything.

MARYAT LEE
AND OONA GIBBS

"I remember you said [orthodoxy] was a ceiling you come through," O'Connor writes Maryat Lee, the words echoing those from Oona Gibbs.[1]

In December 1956 Flannery met Lee, a playwright originally from the South, who was then residing in New York. Many considered Maryat a strange friend for Flannery. Her brother, Robert "Buzz" Lee, was the president of the Georgia State College for Women. One can imagine Lee traipsing through town in a heavy faux-fur coat with hair loose like shredded paper-mache—sometimes with cans of beer in her coat pockets.[2] She would not fit in with the idle young shoppers and mothers with their pinned-up buns and buttoned blouses. The streets are cobbled in Milledgeville. If Maryat strutted down those streets in New York shoes, such as 1960s clogs with plastic soles, one would hear her clapping against the uneven stones. She probably would have been batting away gnats from her face, like unknown choreography, and cursing those barely visible inconveniences.

Maryat was the inspiration for Asbury and Julian, which both she and O'Connor acknowledged in their correspondence. In August 1958, she identifies herself as Asbury from "The Enduring Chill": "The communion with the two n——s, the farce with the priest and the persistent overhand of Knowledge—these are so perfectly close to my own experience of Things, that it seems downright shameful I didn't write it instead of you.

. . . Wishing for an icicle to descend."[3] The story that becomes "Everything That Rises Must Converge" is drawn from Maryat's biography. When she boarded a bus to return North, she spied a Black woman wearing a purple and red Easter hat. Along the route, the bus stopped at a gas station, and Maryat offered to save a seat for the woman. Maryat writes to Flannery: "Half an hour later when we boarded the new bus, the poor woman was way back on the seat of the bus, her hat a little awry and she looked done in."[4] Affronted by Lee's pretentious attempts at cordiality, the woman had moved to the back of the bus. Sarah Gordon notes that O'Connor "appears to use Lee's experience as an essential part of the structure of the story."[5] Lee was the muse for O'Connor's developing interest in writing about social activism and its complications.

As much as Oona's character opposes and rattles Walter's, so Maryat plays the contrarian to Flannery. Lee describes herself in her 1965 journal as the "direct antithesis" to O'Connor:

> I somewhat fascinated her, as she did me, as the direct antithesis of herself, yet someone she nevertheless seemed to care for—in the contrary way which is peculiarly dear to her. She summoned *me*.[6]

Because of O'Connor's and Lee's conflicting natures, many of O'Connor's other friends had difficulty understanding their friendship. James Lewis McLeod, a Milledgeville local, spends pages of his memoir casting around for a motive for why O'Connor would want to associate with Maryat. He settles on the idea that O'Connor intended to convert Maryat as well as use her for material, calling Lee the "perfect grist for Flannery's mill." While McLeod mistakenly views Lee as a "silly self-anointed liberal out to elevate the world while dressed up as a clown,"[7] O'Connor's letters signify more understanding toward Maryat, more "care," as Maryat puts it. In her edition of O'Connor's letters, Sally Fitzgerald notes, "There are no other letters among

Flannery's like those to Maryat Lee, none so playful and so often slambang. . . . Behind all the mockery . . . lay the greatest mutual fondness."[8] Although Asbury and Julian are more cynical appropriations of Lee, Oona becomes a more sympathetic version of O'Connor's friend.

In the letters between Oona and Walter, there are even hints at a love relationship, which parallels at least Lee's devotion to O'Connor. Colleen Warren argues that "for the first time in her fiction," O'Connor was attempting to create "a healthy romantic relationship."[9] Walter does describe his correspondence as "making love through the mail," and Oona several times expresses her driving impetus as "love," despite the fishiness of the word. If we look at the unrequited affection between Maryat and Flannery, we have a sense of how Walter and Oona's romance may have faded into ash. When Lee confesses her love for O'Connor, she is disappointed by O'Connor's response: "Everything has to be diluted with time and matter, even that love of yours which has come down on many of us to be able to come down on one. It is grace and it is the blood of Christ."[10] Lee counters:

> Maybe it is. But of more moment, it is me, my blood and flesh, and heart full. . . . I take you with or without the blood of the lamb, and still it is you I love, and my heart leaps. Oh Flannery, your reply falls pitifully short, a ruse of bones, chill breeze, inadequate, obfuscating, limp, full of clichés, the quaver of a solitary voice in the airless eternities and fog drifting over in sheets.[11]

Prior to writing this letter, Lee had recently married. However, the ties to her spouse did little to restrict her love for others. In addition to professing love for O'Connor, Lee developed what Brad Gooch calls a "one-sided crush" on Donald Ritchie, a film critic she met in Tokyo.[12] All of this occurred less than a year after her marriage began. This biographical parallel does not bode well for a happily ever after for Oona and Walter.

DOCUMENTING "REAL" LIFE

To test Oona's affections further, Walter determines to create a photo journal, which will actually be a series of pictures that portray a performative vision of his life on the farm. If this novel had been written in the twenty-first century, Walter's deception might have taken the form of googling pictures and posting them as his Facebook profile or photoshopping his Instagram selfie. He walks around his parents' property with the intention of finding the most dejected versions of things and showing Oona only this narrow piece of life at Meadow Oaks.

Flannery opines, "Photographers are the lowest breed of men."[1] Walter falls into this category as he stalks the farm taking pictures to lie about what is in front of him. As he tours the farm, he encounters two characters whose plotlines remain unfinished. In an earlier scene between Walter and Mary Maud, Walter insists that his sister will be controlled only by a "large, stupid, demanding man."[2] O'Connor seems to create such a suitor in Boatright, an exemplar of a backward, racist Southerner. This brief scene sets up a future interaction between Mary Maud and Boatright that was, alas, never written.[3] Thankfully Mr. Gunnels, Tilman's field hand, becomes O. E. Parker in "Parker's Back," so we do receive the rest of his story.

Presumption of Knowing

Why Do the Heathen Rage?

PHOTO JOURNAL[1]

He postponed for several days answering the letter, until he should have made up his mind exactly what line to take. He would have to make his double begin to sound more like himself, while at the same time he kept the black aspect before her. Let her get a good look at Roosevelt and her sense of detail would become keener. He had a Brownie camera that he had not used since he was a child. He bought a roll of film, so that he would have a good selection to choose from and then he set out to concoct a picture-story of his life at Meadow Oaks.

All one morning he wandered about snapping scenes here and there. Directly after breakfast, his mother put on her sun hat and threw a smock over her shoulders, took her stick and set out on an inspection tour. Tempers flared in her wake. He followed her with his Brownie at a discreet distance. Halfway toward the barn she stopped as the sound of the small tractor became plain in the distance. In a second Mr. Gunnels, astride the tractor, appeared coming around a bend in the road, heading toward the barn. He had been to an old shell of a house set out in one of the far fields where they stored hay. Every three or four days, he was supposed to take the tractor wagon out there and get a wagonload of hay and take it to the horse stalls where, instead of horses, she kept calves. Mr. Gunnels seemed to hesitate as he came over the hill and saw her, paused in the road, waiting for him. He continued to come forward but at a less enthusiastic pace.

The Gunnels were one of Walter's chief areas of research, though he did it all through his mother. Every night he asked her, "What's the latest on the Gunnels?" and she would answer with a long, detailed recitation, full of sighs and ironical grimaces. She had hired him after Tilman came home from the hospital, and she had seen finally that Walter was never going to be any good to her. Gunnels had described himself in the Market Bulletin as "an expert dairyman, regular churchgoer with 14 years of experience." He turned out to be erratic, careless, resentful, but she handled him very well, using the exact tone with him to maintain his dignity and not more. There were ten Gunnels in all, three children of Mrs. Gunnels by a former marriage, two of his by a former marriage, and three of theirs together. Mrs. Gunnels bordered on obesity; Mr. Gunnels was rail-thin. He had a long Lincoln-like face set between elaborate yellow sideburns.

Walter had seen Gunnels looking at him curiously from a distance as if he might be gazing at a mysterious invalid or someone who was not all there. According to his mother, he had asked her, "How come he don't work? Must be something busted in him," and she had answered, "There is," and let it go at that.

She stood in Gunnels's path, so that he had no alternative but to stop the tractor.

"Good morning, Mr. Gunnels," she said and went directly to the back of the wagon and looked in. She looked for at least thirty seconds, her face stiff with disgust. Then she came back to the tractor and looked Mr. Gunnels directly in the eyes. "Mr. Gunnels," she said, "there are only five bales of hay in that wagon."

Gunnels's shoulders slumped. They were bare and almost entirely covered with tattoos. She had said to him often enough to know that it was of no use, "Mr. Gunnels, I would prefer that you wear a shirt," or "Mr. Gunnels, I expect my colored help to wear shirts, and I expect you to set them the right example." But it was plain that he had not spent his money on these decorations to have them go unseen. Around the barn and in the field, he was always without his shirt. On his chest was a large American eagle mounted on a cannon. A black panther crossed one shoulder and a spotted cat the other. Various serpents coiled about his arms. It was the one on his back which was most offensive to her. It was a large head of Christ. "It's sacrilegious," she said. "It's an offense against religion. And it's ugly, ugly, the ugliest thing you've ever seen. Christ didn't look like that." Walter, hoping to get sight of it, had driven her out to the field one day soon after Gunnels's arrival on the place. He sat in the car while she talked to Gunnels and looked out from the side of a newspaper which he pretended to be reading. When she finished, Gunnels turned and mounted the tractor and swung it around rapidly and was off, the tiller rattling behind him. The face, wet with Gunnels's sweat, was in Walter's view only a second. He had just time to recognize the head of Grunewald's "Crucifixion." On the way back to the house, he ran the car into a ditch and was badly shaken up.

His mother had learned not to look lower than Gunnels's nose, and she stood in front of him now, looking straight into his brownish yellow eyes. "Mr. Gunnels," she said, "I have to pay for the tractor fuel it takes to go out to that field and back and on this load, I've paid for fuel to bring back five bales of hay. I've told you a dozen times if I've told you once to bring back a full wagon load. Now I can't put up with this. No," she said as his mouth started to open, "let me finish what I have to say."

Walter meanwhile had come up close enough to snap a picture of them. Gunnels heard the click and turned his eyes. His posture altered as if he were suddenly sitting a high-spirited horse. The breast of the American eagle on his chest expanded. His long lower jaw extended, and a look of sullen dignity spread over his features.

Mrs. Tilman turned her head. "What are you doing, Walter?" she asked sharply.

"Nothing," Walter said and turned back the way he had come.

She watched his retreating figure suspiciously and then looked back at Gunnels. "I don't want to have to tell you this again," she said.

"No'm," Mr. Gunnels said, but she might have been a speck of dust on the ground; his eyes were on Walter hurrying down the road. He put the tractor in gear and started off after him. When he was about ten feet behind him, he stopped the machine and jumped off of it.

Walter quickened his pace.

"I seen what you was at," Gunnels said. "I never give you no permission to take my picture."

Walter turned. Gunnels was quite close but in the position of someone who can either advance or retreat at a moment's notice. A glaze of belligerence shone from his inquisitive face. "I never tole you you could point no camera at me," he said.

"I was taking her picture," Walter said mildly. "You weren't in it. I'll take one of you now if you want me to."

Gunnels stared at him for a moment. He turned sideways, and then he removed a sack of tobacco and some cigarette papers from his pocket, and while Walter stood there waiting, he poured a little tobacco in one of the papers.

"You can if you want to," he said.

Walter raised the camera to his eye. He waited until the cigarette was completed and Gunnels had placed it, bent downward slightly, in the side of his mouth. Gunnels narrowed his eyes as if he were studying some important mystery and Walter snapped the picture.

"I'll give it to you when it's developed," he said. "So long."

"Hey wait," Gunnels said. "I got something on my back I want you to take. I can't see it without I get two mirrors and I want to see it straight on. It ain't the Jesus I picked out. The fellow that done it had a book of them and this ain't the one I picked out. The bastard tricked me. I'll pay you to take it," he said.

"That ain't necessary," Walter muttered. "Turn around."

Gunnels turned.

Walter's heart began to thump. The face was badly bloody and severe. Walter raised the camera and found it in the lens. He came closer, held by a kind of smarting repulsion and attraction that seemed to pound with a double beat in his blood. His hand veered erratically as he snapped the picture.

"I paid twenty-fi' dollars for that job," Gunnels said, "and I ought to got my money back. If I ever get back to that town I'm going to take this here snap shot and prove it ain't the same one I picked out. Have you took it yet?"

There was no answer, and he turned. Walter was gone. He looked in both directions and caught sight of him, hurrying down the road toward where his old woman had been heading to dress down the n——s for the day. It was plain enough to Gunnels that the fellow had fits. He must have because if there wasn't something wrong with him, the old woman would have put him to work. She hated idleness worse than she hated sin.

By the time he reached the house where the Negroes lived behind the bull pen, Walter's face had dried and he felt as if he had weathered a crisis. A fresh satanic breeze seemed to be blowing through him, and chilling the passions that a few minutes before had threatened to kindle in him. The Negroes' house looked entirely too substantial to serve his purpose. It was unpainted, but it had windows in it, a pleasant porch and a good roof, and it was set back in a lacy grove of chinaberry trees. It would not attract anyone looking for radical poverty.

"Hi-you, Mist Walter?" a high singsong voice called.

He found Alice after a moment, standing at the side of the house, holding a chicken upside down by the feet. She had on a man's grey felt hat and a pair of Eustis' overalls. Her Indian blood showed through in the insolent cast of her eyes, narrowed over her high cheekbones.

"Hello, Alice," he said.

"I reckon you just ramblin, just restin," she said and trilled her formal respectful laugh behind this, indicating as she always did just what they thought of him, a white man supposed to be Somebody who did nothing by day and worked by night at the liquor store.

He did not answer. He had never liked her, even when he was a child. He abruptly cut off to the left and made his way down to and across a bottom and up again into the back pasture where a few dry cows were grazing. He could see, across the pasture and onto the other side of the highway, the rusted tin roof of the shack he wanted to photograph.

The land belonged to a man named Custer Boatright, a crony of Tilman's, who never repaired his property and would keep a Negro— or a white man if he could find one who would take it—in anything that passed for four walls.

Walter started over the pasture, watching his feet. Halfway across he realized there was no gate in this one opening onto the highway. He went on grimly but at the fence he stopped, defeated for the moment as if he were one of the animals it was meant to keep in. Tilman would have pushed down the second wire, pushed up the top one and swung between them in one continuous motion and kept going, his expression still set, his jaw still working on his wad of tobacco, his mind not deflected for an instant from whatever he had been plotting.

Walter looked across the highway at the shack. It sat, window-less in front, about a foot off the bare swept ground. There were two front doors. Three colored children sat in front of it, playing in dirt. He was not close enough to get the kind of picture he wanted. He put the camera on the ground and pushed it through to the other side with his foot. Then he pushed the top strand of wire down and raised his leg behind him. It barely cleared the wire. He swung it over gingerly, then paused with his leg in midair. He cursed softly and after a moment drew the leg back.

Coming very slowly up the highway was a light green mud-spattered car, not of the latest make. It came even closer as its driver sighted Walter who had changed his tactics and was attempting to come through the first and second strands of wire. A hand and leg and his head were through but his trousers were caught, both at the seat and at the knee by sharp points of wire. He balanced there, precariously, crab-like, unable to decide which limb he should put down next. He moved one hand slowly backwards and began to detach the seat of his trousers. As soon as he got this done, he lost his balance and fell through, ripping a triangular piece out of his pants leg. He sat up bleeding at the chin, and reached for the camera.

The driver of the mud-spattered car watched him get up and start across the highway. He drew the car over onto the grass shoulder of the road and stopped it and continued to watch from there.

Walter went up into the yard and snapped a picture of the shack at about twenty feet. He managed to get in both the wash pot and the three children, who were staring at him as if he were their first white man. Tilman would have given them a nickel. Walter did not have this instinct; he only stared back and then managed a nervous smile. A thin light yellow woman appeared in the door, and he turned quickly and started off.

The driver of the mud-spattered car had got out of it and was waiting for him on the edge of the highway, his hands on his hips and his head thrust forward angrily. It was Boatright. He was a plump old man in a limp seersucker suit and a yellowed panama hat; his face was pocked and rutted like a red quartz rock. Walter started violently at the sight of him.

His pale enraged eye was on the camera. "What you taking pictures of my property for?" he said. "Nobody takes pictures of my property without they see me first."

"It's for my sister," Walter blurted out, inspired by panic.

Boatright's furious expression changed. A gleam entered his eyes. Walter had seen this identical gleam as Mary Maud, recognizing his presence with the barest nod, had passed briefly across the porch one day when he was visiting Tilman. He had jumped up and run after her down the stairs, and across the walk, panting, "Allow me to hep you, young lady," and gripping his fingers into her soft upper arm, he had assisted her into her car, grinning and bowing, like a turkey gobbler. Mary Maud had shot off as if a swarm of hornets were after her. "What's your sister want with a picture of my propty?" he asked as if he could already think of several reasons.

Walter's mind was blank. He glanced wildly to the side. His eye fell on the wash pot. "The wash pot," he mumbled. "She wanted her grade to see a wash pot—it's the way they teach them now," he said and smiled lamely.

"It looks like they would have seen a wash pot before," Boatright said suspiciously.

"All n——s have washing machines these days," Walter said, striking just the right note.

The old man's stomach expanded jovially beneath his belt. "Your sister is a smart young woman," he said. "She has the right idea. Certainly, those children ought to see a wash pot. No reason they should grow up thinking the n——s have always had the latest conveniences." He hoisted his pants at the belt and turned and gazed at the black historical object.

"She don't want a picture of it though," he said. "She wants the real thing. I can arrange to have the school bus bring your sister and her children out here to see that wash pot."

"She'd be mighty pleased," Walter said, "particularly since it was your idea."

"The reason I jumped on you," Boatright said, turning back to him, affably, "I thought you might be working for the Atlanta newspapers."

Walter smiled.

"It would be like them to come down here and take a picture of that shack and say it was all that was left of Custer County. And if that had been the case," he said, "I would have busted your camera." He struck Walter affectionately on the shoulder. "Tell your sister," he said, "that I whole-heartedly agree with her method of teaching. Teller I'll see that her children see a real wash pot."

"I'll teller," Walter said.

Boatright squinted thoughtfully at the wash pot. "On second thought," he said, "it might be easier to take it to the children." He hoisted his pants. "Yes," he said and strode over to the yard and across to where the wash pot sat on a charred spot of ground. "What you want for this thing?" he called to the woman in the door. He bent his knees and gripped both hands around the rim of the pot and lifted it slowly about a foot off the ground and then, very flushed in the face, let it rest again. "Come hep me tote this thing," he called to Walter.

Walter came over to the wash pot.

"Take it to the road while I pay this woman," Boatright said and began rooting in his pocket. On his way toward the woman, he stopped and found a nickel for the children. The woman took the two dollars he gave her and said nothing.

Walter carried the pot to the road and waited while Boatright got his car and brought it up. Then they hoisted the wash pot into the trunk. Boatright offered him a lift but he declined. The old man drove off in excellent humor and Walter went home by way of the highway.

He had four more pictures on his film. Tilman and Roosevelt were on the porch. Tilman never had any objection to having his picture taken, but he didn't want Roosevelt in the picture with him.

"Get behind and try to look like you got good sense," he said, "even though you aint."

Roosevelt got behind the chair and stood there, grinning.

"Don't smile," Walter muttered. "I want a sober picture."

"I ain't had no liquor lately," Roosevelt said.

"I mean solemn," Walter said. "Look solemn."

"All he can look like is what he is," Tilman said. "Pure n——."

"Why are you taking pictures?" his mother asked, appearing in the door. "You've torn your pants," she said, looking at him suspiciously.

He pulled her out onto the porch and put the camera in her hand. "Now be nice and stand here," he said. "And take a picture of them, with me here in the background. Just take it. Don't ask a million questions." He got a little behind and to the left of Roosevelt who had sobered up at once as soon as he saw who was going to take the picture.

"You look like a tramp," she said. "If you want me to take this picture, you go put on a coat and tie and change those torn pants."

"The pants won't be in it," Walter said in an irritated voice. "This is not for the newspaper. It's just for me. Just do what I ask you."

"Roosevelt, you sit down," she said.

"No!" Walter shouted. "I want him in it! I want it just like I fixed it. Just take one the way I want it and you can take the rest any way you want to."

"All right," she said, "hold still." She put the camera to her eye. She moved a little to one side and then to the other. "Walter," she said, "you ought to be directly behind your father's chair and Roosevelt behind you if you want him in it."

"Will you for God's sake just take the picture," Walter groaned. "Will you for God's sake just . . ."

"Leave 'em both the way they are and take the picture," Tilman growled between his teeth so as not to change the expression on his face, an expression of being about to render a shattering decision.

She snapped the picture. Walter leaned against the side of the house and wiped his face with the tail of his shirt.

The pictures came back from the photographers all clear except the one of Gunnels's back. On that one Walter's hand had veered. The face was visible but as through a veil. Walter stuck them in the back of his desk drawer and then turned his mind to composing a documented answer to Oona Gibbs.

THE REVOLTING CONVERSION

I've visited Andalusia, O'Connor's home, numerous times. From O'Connor's front window two robust trees gesture with their lengthy arms toward the pond. The red dirt entry to the farm is also visible, and beyond it, the pond itself. Although glossed with algae, the pond looks inviting. You could walk between the cut of woods and across its waters. They used to sell vials of pond water in the store set up in the entryway for tourists, which made me laugh, as though these vials held holy water by which to remember one's pilgrimage to an uncanonized saint's former dwelling. The outside porch is screened in, a segue between the air-conditioned paradise and the infernal heat of the farm. Rather than the colonnades that adorn most antebellum-style plantation houses, this 1930s farmhouse greets visitors with white banisters lining the red brick porch.

Her room has been restored to how she left it: a flat twin bed like a monk might use, with her aluminum crutches leaning against the wardrobe and a Royal typewriter still and silent, waiting for inspiration. When O'Connor describes Walter's room, it sounds similar to how her own room may have appeared:

> Everything was mammoth and steady—the black antique high-boy, the giant wardrobe, the old rolltop desk, each stood there like a Grandstaff ancestor who had taken this form for eternity. The desk was large and littered, almost a replica of the room

itself, which was lined with books and papers, all in total disarray, piled evenly on the bed and under it. He would not allow anyone in to clean up. Silver fish darted from between papers and disappeared again. There was a dense network of spider webs connecting the desk to the nearest bookcase.[1]

When I edited the manuscript, witnessing her many rewrites of the opening lines, I imagined Flannery in this bedroom working, fingers perched above the keys of her typewriter and waiting for the clicking symphony to begin. If only she could get the opening sentence right. The pause is drawn out until the silence speaks to the author. "The day the woman descended upon them," Flannery would type, "Walter was upstairs in his room, sitting at his typewriter, finishing a letter to her."[2]

Flannery may have heard a peacock's trill from the yard: a high vibrating sound followed by three or four caws in succession. Then a mower would start to hum, and the call would be drowned out by the mower's modulating buzz. She would have withdrawn the paper from the typewriter to edit by hand. With fingers likely aching from sharp pangs at her joints, Flannery crosses out "woman" and writes "girl." Unsatisfied, Flannery crosses out more words on the sheet: "The day the ~~woman~~ girl descended ~~upon~~ them, Walter was ~~upstairs~~ in his room, ~~sitting at his typewriter, finishing a~~ writing her a letter ~~to her.~~" Still too many words, apparently. She would roll the paper through the typewriter again and return the carriage to the starting position.

> The girl descended on them, a little before noon, rattling up the corrugated clay road in a small red automobile that raised a cloud of angry pink dust behind it. At ten in the morning Walter had been in his room, furiously typing her a letter.

"Rattling?" Her voice was high-pitched and nasally. "Rattling full speed?" The heat of summer may have filled her room like someone else's presence. The apparition of Walter appears lounging on her unmade bed, one moccasin foot perched on top of the other, reading a volume by Romano Guardini.

"Trail of *rust-colored* dust or cloud of pink? Is 'angry' too much?" Her thoughts may have been voiced, but no one inside the house could overhear them.

"Bring her on, Walter, or head her off?" she queries the imaginary entity who appears so comfortable and slothful on her twin mattress. "Neither you nor I know right now, do we?"

Thirty-eight-year-old Flannery O'Connor worked on the start of the story for months, rewriting this opening paragraph almost a dozen times. She continues, of course, to finish out the scene, but it plays over and over again in the same way. Well, almost the same way—whether Walter should encourage the visit of Oona Gibbs or whether he should dissuade her from coming alters from draft to draft. What changes Walter's mind is his sudden—but undramatic—conversion to Christianity.

———————

The conversion scenes for Walter all take place on a rock where he sits reading Oona's letter. There is sacramental significance to the location (Jesus says, "On this rock, I will build my church," Matt. 16:18). But the scene feels strikingly unlike an O'Connor moment of grace. No guns, no murder, no drowning, no goring bulls, no violence whatsoever. In a 1960 letter, O'Connor writes Andrew Lytle: "I keep seeing [Elijah] in that cave waiting to hear the voice of the Lord in the thunder and lightning and wind, and only hearing it finally in the gentle breeze, and I feel I'll have to be able to do that sooner or later, or anyway keep trying."[3] With Walter's conversion to belief, O'Connor attempts to recall the biblical passage, 1 Kings 19, in which Elijah hears the voice of God.

The moment sounds similar to C. S. Lewis's conversion. O'Connor was reading quite a few Lewis books in her last years. After almost three hundred pages into his autobiography, *Surprised by Joy*, Lewis describes the effects of books on the cultivation of his imagination, depicting a rather humdrum scene of converting to Christianity. He writes:

> When we set out I did not believe that Jesus Christ is the son of God, and when we reached the zoo I did. Yet I had not exactly spent the journey in thought. Nor in great emotion. "Emotional" is perhaps the last word we can apply to some of the most important events. It was more like when a man, after a long sleep, still lying motionless in bed, becomes aware that he is now awake.[4]

Lewis does not explain why or exactly how he came to believe, but only that it happened, the way one opens one's eyes after a night's sleep.

Walter's conversion reads similarly. After concluding that Oona has abrogated the place of God, he realizes that he must believe in God:

> He had not up until that moment been a believer. But he realized then, with a shudder that he was. He was a Christian, bound for hell. His throat had gone instantly dry, his face had grown pale, and it had looked as if the countryside had dropped away from the rock he had sat on, and he and the rock were suspended over nothing. Walter knew the Fathers of the Church, he had assisted at Nicaea and at Chalcedon. He had explored the intricacies of Light with Bonaventure; he knew where Aquinas and Duns Scotus would part company. He had seen the path turn downward with Abelard and illogic enter, grandly eloquent, with Luther. He had been active at Trent. He had adhered always to the most orthodox line but never once, never for the slightest moment, had it occurred to him, even remotely, to believe any of it; or that there was the least danger of his doing so. Only now it simply appeared the accomplished truth. Grace originated elsewhere and grace was. It mattered and worse, the woman mattered.[5]

This scene is rewritten four times, and each time, Walter determines to rid himself of Oona, to cease the correspondence and keep her from coming to visit.

Why Do the Heathen Rage?

DO NOT COME, OONA GIBBS![1]

W alter kept turning the airmail letter over in his hand. He had spent considerable time over his reply and had torn up several letters before he struck the tone he wanted to adopt. This was one of cynical intelligent despair. He wrote the girl that he was in a peculiar position to understand her philosophy, but that it was impossible to put it into practice in a section where selfishness was so much a way of life that it could no longer be recognized as such. There was enough truth in this to make the writing of it disagreeable to him and it was, at the same time, enough of a lie to justify his treating it as a joke.

Across the lawn Walter saw Roosevelt on his knees at his mother's feet. He had apparently cut a bulb with his hoe and she was making him pick them out by hand after he had loosened the dirt a little with the trowel. She stood over him with her hands on her hips. The Oppressor, Walter thought, and smiled.

"I want Roosevelt," Tilman said suddenly. "I want to go to the bathroom. Get him here quick."

This was a ruse to get the Negro away from his wife. Walter cupped his hands to his mouth and shouted across the lawn, "Daddy wants Roosevelt!"

"Goddamit," the old man wheezed, "go get him, or I ain't going to wait."

Walter jumped up and ran across the grass. "Daddy wants Roosevelt quick," he said. "He threatens action." His mother sighed.

"He's been already this morning, hasn't he, Roosevelt?" she said.

"No'm, he ain't," the Negro murmured.

"I've told you not to bring him out until he has," she said sharply. "Well, go on. You're a pack of children. Nothing ever gets done on this place."

Roosevelt raised himself slowly and ambled off toward the porch.

"He's spoiled that n—— to death," she said. "He's not worth shooting." She squatted down and pulled her dress over her knees and began to work with the trowel. "Of course, you could help me do this," she said, "if you're not going anywhere." Walter lowered himself reluctantly. He got up a bulb and then stopped. "Listen," he said, "there may be company. A woman I write to threatens to come this direction. I've tried to head her off but I have an idea she won't be headed."

"Well," his mother said, "I think it's nice for you to have your friends."

"I didn't invite her. This isn't my idea. You won't like her."

"I can get along with anybody," his mother said. "I'm sure she's nothing she shouldn't be," she added, looking up suddenly into his face as if she were not so sure as she said she was.

"I never met her," Walter said vaguely. "Somebody I write to. I'm still trying to head her off. I just want to warn you though. I may not be successful."

"Well, try to be successful," his mother said. "We really don't need any company right now. What does this girl do?"

Walter groaned. "She's uh, she's uh, kind of uh—social worker only not. She's kind of a fanatic."

"I don't argue religion with anybody," his mother said.

"Not a religious fanatic," Walter said. "A kind of radical."

She gave him an alarmed look. "A communist?"

"No'm," he said, "not that, but I told you, I ain't met her."

"Well, I just hope she's not trashy," his mother said. "You ought to be more careful of the people you get involved with. Just because they have brains doesn't mean they're nice people." She had already come to the conclusion that Walter's only salvation would be to marry a woman who could take over for him. She had been looking for someone for him like herself, aware that women are not made like herself anymore and that she would have to settle for something else.

"Is this girl married or single?" she asked.

"Single, I suppose," Walter said. "What's the difference?"

"Just be careful," his mother said. "She may be after you. She may be some kind of siren, and you are very innocent, Walter. You could easily be taken in."

"Oh, for God's sake," Walter muttered, but his face turned a darker pink. The fact was, it was plain to him that she *was* after him, but the poor girl was in for a surprise. She thought he was a Negro.

His image of her now after three months of steady correspondence varied violently. Behind his absent gaze at his mother, Walter was parting a shower of pink gold hair, dividing it upon a back bare its length, then bending to kiss exactly the hollow of it, exactly the spot best suited to receive first his lips and then his cheeks. Walter took the letter out of his pocket and stared for a moment at the address. His mother looked at it with an exasperated face.

"Look," Walter said. Tilman and Roosevelt had not moved from the porch.

"I told you," she said, not even looking up.

She understood Tilman perfectly. She knew his drives. She knew exactly how his mind worked. She had always been prepared with her own cunning to counter his, and in spite of his orneriness, she respected him. She respected him the way it is possible to respect a man who knows what he wants and works to get it. But how was it possible to respect Walter? All Walter knew about the land was that it was underneath him.

His mother plunged the trowel into the ground and brought up a mound of dirt which she slung to the side. "When is she coming?" she asked in a resigned tone.

"I don't know," Walter said. "I hope she won't arrive at all. I just wanted to warn you." He felt his face grow warm at this lie. The letter in his hand was an invitation, a reckless impassioned plea for her to come. She was visiting Fellowship Farm, and it was only seventy miles away, a blight squarely in their midst. Walter would never have ventured into the infected area himself, but he wanted to see the girl, separated from her fellows; he wanted to clear his mind of her once and for all.

His mother lifted the letter from his hand before he realized what she was doing and read the address. Her mouth pursed. She looked at him squint-eyed as if he appeared to her a monstrosity and capable of anything. "Walter," she hissed, "you wouldn't bring one of those people here?"

"She isn't one of them," he said hastily. "She's only visiting there. That's why I'm afraid she'll come on by here."

"What kind of person," she asked coldly, "would *want* to visit there?"

Walter was silent.

"Walter," she said, "you've never seen this woman. You don't even know whether she's white or black."

"She couldn't be black," he murmured. But he saw that she could be huge and vulgar and emaciated and loud and brash—the letters admitted of anything. She had not sent him the pictures of herself that he had asked for. He turned his face slightly away from the cutting eyes in front of him. A parade of horrors passed before him. For the first time, he conceived of her as simple flesh, and he sickened. The letter in his hand was an invitation, a plea, a cry from the heart to come and come quickly to someone who needed help. Without thinking he snatched the letter from his mother's hand and tore it in two.

"Were you *asking* this woman to come here?" his mother murmured in an incredulous tone.

Walter's face was now a violent red.

"No," he said, "I was trying to head her off, but I think I know a stronger way to do it." He was already on his feet.

"Well, use the stronger way," she said. "And don't get yourself in such a mess again."

He started off headlong toward the house, and she stopped what she was doing and watched him until he was up the steps and disappeared through the front door. He had been acting more and more peculiar lately—much more peculiar than he was to begin with. She was not a woman given to tears, but there is no affliction like children who fail. Her eyes felt hot and hard and she closed them. It was the way the world was, but the world was still remote from Meadow Oaks.

They read about it in the papers, and they watched it on television, but nothing terrible happened here. The sorrows here were muted and well-known and dependable. There was nothing to startle you. Even Walter did not startle her; he gave her no more than dull grief, like a child with an unknown lingering disease. There was no violence. The government was not threatening to put a highway through the place. The Negroes were shiftless and secretive and resentful, but they worked for what you could pay them, and they still cut each other, not their white people. If it had not been the way the children had turned out, there would only have been a few things to tell you that these were not her father's times, you would not have guessed that everything was wrong underneath, that nothing was really what it seemed. With a harried expression, she returned to her digging.

Once in his room, Walter sat down in dread to compose a new letter. The desk was large and littered, almost a replica of the room itself, which was lined with books and papers, all in total disarray, piled evenly on the bed and under it. He would not allow anyone in to clean up. Silver fish darted from between papers and disappeared again. There was a dense network of spider webs connecting the desk to the nearest bookcase. His room was in the back part of the house and looked out over the chicken yard and a series of sheds.

His horror at himself was as dark as his fear that Oona Gibbs would come. His vicissitudes of feeling about the woman, his imbecilic tempting of fate, his idiot behavior all spring—all of it had to do with the ugly fact of his discovered belief, of his revolting conversion which he had neither been able to throw off or warm up. Unlike Paul he had not been thrown to the ground and blinded; he saw as well or better than ever. His vision was as clear as Satan's. It was his will that was out of kilter. His taste had gone bad. His appetites had become voracious, and fantasy would not sate them.

He cursed the day he had written her in the first place. In the most formal terms Walter begged Oona's pardon for all the letters, which had been a hoax prompted by a complete absence of admiration for the movement and her article about it. He wanted to wash his hands of her quickly and thoroughly. The discovery that had transformed her from a caricature into a human being had increased his repulsion proportionately. A letter would not reach her in time. He would need to send a telegram.

He grabbed his pen and jotted down on the back of an envelope, "Mother dying. Do not come. Walter Tilman." In a second, he scratched out "Mother" and wrote "Father." Then he groaned as he realized that would certainly not stop her. That would only be a further invitation. She would have the excuse of coming where she was needed. Guilt fastened upon him, and he felt the thorn in his side of his discovered belief. He scratched out "Father." After a moment, he wrote, "INFECTIOUS HEPATITIS. DO NOT COME." This had more promise. She would probably not advance in the face of infection.

He wondered if hepatitis was heinous enough. She might not know what it was. He scratched it out and wrote "Spinal meningitis" above it. But if he had spinal meningitis, he could not get up to send the telegram, and he would have to sign his mother's name. With infectious hepatitis, he could probably have got to the telephone to send the wire. He decided upon infectious hepatitis, added "VERY DANGEROUS. Do not come. Walter Tilman."

His own venality depressed him. He got up and went to the upstairs extension telephone, which was in the hall not far from his room and called in the telegram. When he finished, he continued to sit on the small stool, very hot, exhausted, staring into the guest room across from his own—the room which, if the girl came, she would occupy.

That night he dreamed about her. She was driving a red convertible filled with Negroes in bathing trunks—they were all on the way to the beach. Walter tore after them until he was somehow there driving with the girl, hanging about his neck, screaming directions into his ear, and the Negroes stamping their feet rhythmically on the floor of the speeding car. Walter awoke breathless.

She was even then only sixty miles away, speeding forward as deadly and innocent as a flame in her little red automobile.

INTRODUCING THE GIRL

Readers do not get much of Oona Gibbs in the unfinished manuscripts, and what they receive seems like episodes from the lives of several different women. Is Oona Gibbs based on the compassionate but occasionally exploitative and always theatrical Maryat Lee? Or is she a pathetic figure—sometimes called Sarah in the drafts—with little education, struggling between submitting to her overbearing mother and being her own person? In a handful of pages, Sarah is introduced in conversation with her mother, who seems more like Oona Gibbs than Sarah does, and who alludes to being a relation to Walter, perhaps his aunt. We do not receive enough clues about the ways in which these figures fit with Walter's story or how it would have all come together after years of workshopping by O'Connor.

However, the girl is worth meeting, with all her complexities and mysteries. Her mother, the existentialist activist, poses an interesting contrast to the hardworking farm women of many of O'Connor's stories. By witnessing their interactions and listening in on their dialogue, readers receive hints of what worried O'Connor when it came to activism of a certain brand. Interlacing the leftover scenes together, the girl speeding toward Walter's home that fated day is slowed down and her motivations filled out a little more. Who is Oona Gibbs?

See Me

Why Do the Heathen Rage?

THE GIRL[1]

The girl descended on them a little before noon, rattling up the corrugated clay road in a small red automobile that raised a trail of pink dust behind it. A mile before the girl reached the place, her heart had begun to thump with a sharp erratic beat like a wild ferreting creature that sensed danger or delight when no sign was apparent to her. She drove a few hundred yards farther and then pulled the car off the highway onto the shoulder. She sat gripping the steering wheel, staring out over a pasture where black and white cows were grazing. Beyond the pasture a green wood rose on a hill; beyond that the distant tree line was black and jagged. The girl was breathing asthmatically.

"You only live once," she muttered.

Her head was wrapped around with a flowered headscarf under which there were large curlers. She took off the scarf and began absentmindedly to remove the curlers, letting down long strands of plain brown hair. She had a thin face pinched in about the nose, and her lower jaw hung just a little slack as if she were in the habit of breathing through her mouth. Nothing distinguished the face but its look of not taking in enough air. Her eyes were green and pale.

She looked again at the trees on the hill and found the red roof of the house. It must be a tall house. She could see only one patch of white under the roof that was not hidden by green. It was a tin roof; the sun almost directly over it was reflected in one round bright spot a little to the left of a barely visible television aerial. Her sense of being in an alien place subsided a little as she made out the aerial. They heard the same news everyone else heard; they were advised to use the same soap and buy the same cars.

"Do something, for God's sake," her mother had always said. "Do something even if it's wrong. When I was your age I'd been in jail three times. I had a lover. I'd published a poem. I cared about humanity. Listen, if my leg wasn't swollen as big as my head, I'd be in Mississippi right now, or Birmingham or Albany, or in Texas doing something about those wet-backs. I'd rot for what I believed in."

Her mother sat most of the day at the front window, looking down on the corner of Riverside Drive and 110th Street, her swollen leg stretched out in front of her. Except for the leg, she was thin and drawn. Her eyes burned a black blue in her white face. "Instead, here I sit rotting for nothing," she would say in a harsh, low, furious voice and her gaze would rove, outraged, over the large nearly empty room. There was nothing in it but their chairs and a library table strewn with books and papers and medicine bottles. Until the illness became advanced, they had sat on the floor, Japanese style. Then they were forced to buy a chair. Her mother got painfully into a taxi and they went to a second-hand furniture dealer's. Her mother took grim satisfaction in picking out the most ridiculous chair in the place. It was a straight one, partially but not too stuffed, with turned-out lion's paws for feet and arms, and a fluted back with a lyre at the top. The upholstery was green plush like that on the seats in old Pullman cars. They bought at the same time a cane-bottomed straight chair for the swollen leg to rest on and another for Oona herself. They bought second-hand things because they were contemptuous of money, not because they lacked it.

"There ought to be something," Oona said, sitting on her straight chair in the tentative awkward way she sat on it with her hand gripped in the seat and her arms stiff, "that you could rot for here. I mean like, well, I mean suffering ought to come to something." She began to grow red at the idiocy of this before she had got through saying it.

"Oh, for God's sake, Oona, stop that kind of stupid talk," her mother said. "When I die, God knows what'll happen to you. You'll go to work in an insurance office probably. And join the church. Methodist, I should say. And sing in the choir." Her voice tightened. "I've done the best I could for you but now my life is over."

It had been over, but she kept herself ready for it to begin again. She had her hair dyed and bobbed every three months, and as she sat in her chair, she worked certain muscles to keep them in condition. She was only fifty-four, looked forty-five, and smelled of cancer. She always told Oona that life was unfair, but the girl assumed she meant it was unfair to the poor and oppressed, not to well-off people contemptuous of money who took up for the poor and oppressed, as she and her mother had always done. Now she saw that it was unfair even to the good, and even to those like herself who were neither good nor bad, one thing or the other, just nothing in particular. There was no one to blame. All you could say was that life was unfair.

Some days her mother felt a wild energy racing through her. Oona would roll a little table over the arms of her chair and put the typewriter on it, and her mother would burn out her passion for fifteen or twenty minutes writing. Then she would be nauseated and push it away and after that she would sink into a kind of cold, shut-mouthed indifference. They read together, aloud, a book about a man who committed suicide with his wife's help rather than put up with the death that faced him. The girl felt conflicting things about the book. She felt it was noble to control your own destiny that way, but her feelings about it were not as strong as she thought they should have been. Her emotions seldom met her expectations. Her mother said, "That was all right for him, but not for me."

"I'd help you if you wanted me to," the girl said.

"Ha," her mother laughed. "You would shake and change your mind in the middle of it. No, that's not for me. I mean to stay to the end and spit in his eye."

"Spit in whose eye?" the girl asked.

"In the eye of death," her mother said. "God, you have no imagination."

The pasture that the girl now looked out on was dotted here and there with wild pink poppies. She noticed that the cows had lifted their heads and were looking with a steady animal attention at her car. One or two were moving forward toward the barbed wire fence. She knew nothing about cows but the fence looked as if it would hold them. She looked down into her lap and there were the curlers. She removed a comb from the purse at her side and began roughly to comb her hair out straight. Trying to make herself look more at-tractive was dishonest. Her policy for the last three weeks was to be as plain as she was, to live on the most radical and barest existential level. She asked nothing of life but experience; she demanded nothing of herself but an absolutely truthful response to it. She had written this down in a kind of manifesto and she repeated it to herself several times a day like a prayer in time of temptation. "I exist. Nothing mat-ters but absolute honesty. I will look for the absolute core of truth in every human being I meet. I will not be frightened. There is nothing to be frightened of." There were several rubber bands hanging on the door handle. She removed one and secured her hair behind her neck with it. The cows continued to watch the car as if they were warily considering it for food.

Now turn around and go back where you came from, a silence inside her said. The devil exists, and you are attracting his atten-tion. This was the voice of temptation, in her like an undertow. It was against this that she repeated her prayer. A little chill passed over her, and her skin prickled. "I exist," she said. "Nothing matters but absolute honesty." In her right mind, her mother would have approved of what she was doing.

She was twenty-four years old now. On coming of age, she had felt a sudden fragile blossom of youth and a faint gentle but unmistakable power as if she were Merlin growing backwards and had reached her prime. She took a peculiar literal-minded pride in the abstraction, "of age." It conferred a dignity on her that she had not experienced before. But she saw that it was a state that would not last long. Age would follow it soon or rather age would close back around it, for she had always been old. She had been an asthmatic ancient child and more ancient still in adolescence. When she had come into her own, she felt the power of owning something. There was a lot of it. It came to her from her father's will. She had never seen him, but he had felt enough responsibility for his act to provide a lump sum on her twenty-first birthday.

Her mother had always said, "You are the product of a free act not a legal bondage, so act like it."

She lost the roof of the house in a blur of green; the black and white cows ran together. Her chin trembled and she gasped for breath for she could not weep and breathe at the same time. Her face grew dark. She reached blindly for a handkerchief out of the purse and blew her nose hard and then sat with her head laid back and her mouth open. The tears appeared to burn dry in her red-rimmed eyes.

At the end, their roles had been reversed. Oona herself was the one who stood up for what they believed in. She was the one with the strong mind and the firm will. Her mother became nothing but a child. Her sight failed first, then her mind. The first day her mother was blind, she sat with a look of horror on her face, her black eyes torn in their depths. When her sight returned, she settled into some deep blank indifference, as if she were practicing death. Then she went blind again and began to whimper and cry to go home. She gave Oona directions to pack their suitcases and call the railroad station and reserve the berths, to get an ambulance to take them to the station and another to meet the train. The girl sat most of the time on her straight chair at the window, her head folded on her arms. She wished they were both dead. Her mother screamed and raged when she understood that nothing was being done, that nothing was going to be done.

The girl hung over her, trying to goad her into being herself. Unasked, she began to read the Bhagavad Gita. She liked the noble rhythm and the soft illusion of God in it.

"Stop that!" her mother said. "Stop that for God's sake."

"You used to like it."

"I said stop it, didn't I?"

"Why don't you want me to read?"

"Nothing. Let me alone." There were dark circles under her eyes and in the pupils, there seemed to be little pits of darkness opening up. "I want to go home," she muttered.

"Don't pay any attention to what you think now," Oona said, "because whatever you're thinking now it's because you're sick and I'm not going to let you do anything you wouldn't want to do if you were . . . all right." She had an idea, more fanciful than her ideas usually were. Her eyes brightened. "You're like Ulysses tied to the mast, see, and I'm the dumb sailors with wax in their ears so they can't hear the singing and be led off the right course. See?" she said, delighted at being able to make something, for once, so plain.

Her mother said nothing. Her face was absolutely hard, expressionless. She seemed not even to have heard.

"Don't you see?" Oona said uneasily.

"I want my reward," her mother said.

"Reward?" the girl murmured. "Reward for what?"

"For a good life," her mother said, "ha ha."

The girl sat there stupidly. She never understood her mother's jokes.

"All my life I've spent either doing good for other people or fighting for their rights and this is my reward."

"We are above rewards," Oona said. "We only do things because they're right."

"I want my reward," her mother said, gritting her teeth. "I want it like a child wants candy. I want it. I want it."

If Oona had not come of age, she could not have been steadfast. She would have done what she was told. She would have let her mother in her last moments make a fool of herself. She saw that all of her life had been a preparation for this. Her real mother was already dead. The distraught woman who screamed at her was not real. It came to her only slowly that she should kill this woman and herself. Her mother could spit in the eye of a quick death as easily as a prolonged one, and as for herself, it would be more honorable than working in an insurance office and joining the church and the choir. She realized that she had been born only for a few little moments of courage and nobility.

There were no great oaks in the pasture Oona saw before her now, but she did not suppose that she was very close to the house. She looked again for the roof and when she found it, it appeared to be actually on a second hill, or maybe a third. Walter had written that after she turned off the highway, she would drive two miles on a dirt road, then turn to the right onto a narrower private road; the house was a quarter of a mile down this. She pictured an avenue of oaks leading up to a white house with columns. A kind of a cliché of a Southern house. Walter said it was "antebellum as hell."

There were four or five such houses in the little towns she had passed through and she had resented them, or at least she had resented the ones that were well-painted and kept up. The others, grey with black rotted sills, she was able to pity. But this one, couched mysteriously in woods, she resented most of all, because it was where he suffered. She would not be welcome there, except by him. And not, it seemed, by him, outwardly, only inwardly.

From the open purse, she removed a snapshot and began to study it. It showed the white family on the porch with him standing behind the old man's wheelchair bent over the invalid so that the round top of his head and not his face was visible. The old man apparently had no teeth, but he nevertheless looked, to her, fierce and vicious. He had on his hat, but he was obviously not going anywhere. A cane stretched across his knees. The son was standing between the two of them, leaning against the side of the house with his hands behind him. He had a kind of noncommittal superior half-smile on his face. He was large and slovenly, prematurely balding but the picture of self-satisfied indifference.

The girl's gaze returned to the Negro attendant and remained there for some time on the bent shoulders and bowed head. He had on an orderly's white jacket and one black hand was on the arm of the wheelchair, which he had apparently been adjusting to the old man's specifications.

All along the way, she had tried to feel what her mother, in her right mind, would have felt. Years after her mother's death, the voice was still with her.

"I want it," her mother wailed. "I want my reward. I want to go home, oh I want to go home, let me go home, please let me go home."

The doctor came reluctantly when Oona called him. He had come only the day before and knew there was no sense in another visit. Oona met him at the elevator and began.

"She's raving. She's out of her head," she said, beginning to whimper at the sight of him.

"She's not out of her head," he repeated. His thumb was flattened on the elevator button. "She may live two or three more weeks. Get her a minister or a priest or something."

The girl smiled proudly. "She's not that out of her head. She's above any kind of cheap comfort or any lie."

The doctor jammed his finger down on the button three times in rapid succession. "Nothing can comfort her because there is no comfort," Oona said.

There was a whine and the elevator door opened. He bolted in and was swallowed downward out of her sight.

When she went back into the room, her mother had pulled herself erect. She was gripping both arms of the chair as if she intended to stand. "He said I might have three weeks. I'm going home," she said. "Call up the railroad station and get us berths and get an ambulance to take us to the station and have them arrange for another ambulance to meet the train, then get out the suitcases and pack one for both of us, that's all we need. I'm not going to notify them. I'm just going to arrive."

The girl stood for a moment doing nothing, her face twisted as if some minor convulsion were taking place behind it. She took her straight chair and pulled it by the knob at the top over to the window.

Then she sat down and folded her arms on the window ledge and put her face down on them. The sun was warm on the top of her head, like a hand held there. "I wish we were both dead," she said.

That night after supper, the girl washed her face and combed her hair and put on a clean dress, a white one she had never worn before. She had pulled the sheet off her bed and taken it to her mother's chair. Her mother had fallen into a fitful sleep. She tied her to the chair with the sheet. When her mother woke up, the girl was sitting facing her with a kitchen knife in her lap. It took her a few seconds to perceive she was tied up.

"What's this?" she said. "Why do you have this sheet around me? Why do you have your good dress on? What's the knife for in your lap?"

"I don't know how to say it," the girl said. Her face was flushed and expectant.

"Say what?" her mother muttered.

"Well, I'm of age now. Things are really up to me."

Something moved in the depths of her mother's eyes. "You won't help me to go home," she said. "Why have you got me tied up? Are you afraid I'll get away?" She laughed harshly.

"What we believe in," the girl said, "there's nobody to uphold it but me."

"Untie me," her mother said. "I'm helpless enough."

"I'm capable of doing something great," the girl said softly. "It's always been you that did it, but now you can't, and I can. I'm not going to see you suffer or forget yourself or anything. You can spit in the eye of a quick death as well as any other."

Her mother remained absolutely still, her eyes on the girl's face. "Untie me," she said in a sudden peremptory voice.

Oona trembled, but she smiled and shook her head.

"I want you to be proud of me—for once," she said.

"All you want is to get rid of me, so you can enjoy yourself," her mother said. "You can't wait two weeks."

"You know that's not true," the girl said. "I'm going to do you and then I'm going to do me. I want it to sort of be your reward—seeing me do something that takes courage. Don't you see," she said eagerly, "how *right* it is?"

"You can't get out of that," the girl said in a voice on the edge of tears. "It's tied tight."

"I'm not trying to get out," her mother said. "It is just."

"Just?" the word had, to the girl, a false, severe ring.

"Just," her mother said. She turned to face her again. "Have you left a note saying what you are going to do?"

"Why should I leave a note?"

"You are about to commit murder."

"I don't call it murder," the girl said.

"Regardless of what you call it," her mother said, "it is murder. Somebody else might be electrocuted for it."

The girl reddened. "Oh," she said. After a second she got up and went to the library table on the other side of the room and sat down. As soon as her back was turned, her mother began a fierce, silent struggle to unloosen the sheet, lifting one shoulder and then the other. Her face grew red with exertion as she tried to force her arms outward.

"Who to address it to?" Oona asked.

"The police," her mother said.

"What to say?" the girl muttered.

"I'm not going to tell you everything," her mother said.

After a minute Oona wrote, "To the police department:" and then stopped. She was not clever. She had not even been clever enough to get into the good college her mother had wanted to send her to, but she wanted to be able to say something that would have dignity and greatness about it. She sat staring in front of her. Finally, she wrote, "I am about to kill my mother and myself. No one is responsible but me. She is ill and about to die anyway, and I am of age and have the courage it takes to do this. Yours truly, Oona Gibbs." She read it over. It had no dignity, but it was sufficient to keep somebody out of the electric chair. She turned back to her mother, who was trying to ease downward and get out of the sheet that way.

"Loosen this thing," she said and stiffened her hands, so the girl could see that the circulation was cut off. "You're trying to kill me, not torture me to death."

"There's no use loosening it," the girl said. "I'm ready now." And she stood in front of her mother holding the knife ineffectually in her left hand.

"You are not ready," her mother said with an angry smile. "You've forgotten something else."

"Oh, God, what?" the girl cried. "You make me so nervous! You can't even let me do this right." She began to cry openly, and she sat down in the chair and moved the kitchen knife from hand to hand.

"You've forgotten the money you have now," her mother said.

She looked at her mother strangely and stopped moving the knife from one hand to the other. "You just want to live," she murmured. "Since when has money meant anything to us. All it means to me is that he knew I was alive. I wouldn't use it."

"Somebody else could. Think of the people you could help with that money."

The girl stared hopelessly out the window into the blurred streaked lights of the Jersey shore. She felt age close back around her.

"The least you can do," her mother said, "is to make a will and leave that money to somebody who needs it."

"I don't know anybody that needs it," the girl said in a suffocated voice.

"My God!" her mother said. "Half the world is starving."

"I don't know half the world," she muttered.

Her mother's hands crossed awkwardly at the bottom of the sheet were blue and swollen-looking.

"Loosen this please," she said.

The girl got up and fumbled with the knot she had made, but her fingers were too weak to untie it. She cut it with the knife and the sheet fell off around her mother's knees. Her mother rubbed her wrists briefly and then caught her by the arm before she could move away. She pulled her around the side of the chair and sat her down, without letting go of her arm. Then, she leaned forward and shook her slightly. "Listen to me," she said. "Look at me and listen." The girl turned her eyes listlessly toward her. "Suicide is a sin," her mother said and increased the pressure on her arm. "A mortal sin. If you kill yourself, you'll go to hell."

The girl's mouth opened slowly. "Why are you saying that?" she murmured.

"Because it's true," her mother said. "And it's the way you talk to children. And you are a child. I want to save you. I've made a mess of it because I've always talked to you as if you were an adult. Now, I'm going to begin again."

"Don't tell me," the girl said bitterly, "what you don't believe yourself. It's too late to talk to me as if I'm a child. I'm of age."

"I'm telling you the truth," her mother said.

"All I'm worth," the girl said, "is to work in an insurance office and join the church and believe in hell. That's what you think."

"I don't want you to kill yourself," the mother said. "I want you to live and be happy."

"I'll be happy when I'm nothing," the girl said. "Dead. Then I'll be happy. I'll be happy when I stick that knife in myself. Then I'll be happy. I'll be happy when I . . ."

Her mother began to shake her roughly. "Your sin will be on me," she said. "Because you don't know what sin is. But I'm trying to tell you."

WHO IS OONA GIBBS?

Mother, Daughter, Aunt, Cousin, or Lover

The episode between Oona and her mother is disturbing, not only because of its incomplete ending and its hints at murder but also because of its connection to the humanitarian aims of the two characters. Oona mentions a book that she and her mother read aloud "about a man who committed suicide with his wife's help rather than put up with the death that faced him."[1] This book incites Oona's impulse to kill her mother. Most likely, O'Connor is referencing Lael Tucker Wertenbaker's memoir about her husband's suicide, *Death of a Man*, which was published in 1957. Since O'Connor wrote this episode in the 1960s, the debates about euthanasia have become more prominent in the public sphere.

Oona's love is too abstract to bring about real good and, in the end, may be used to justify violence, as it does toward her mother. One should read O'Connor's argument in her introduction to *A Memoir of Mary Ann*, a collection of anecdotes about the life, suffering, and death of a young orphan who resided at a cancer home run by Catholic sisters. O'Connor claims in that introduction that love, without a foundation in the incarnate, crucified God, will lead to greater suffering. Her thesis: "In the absence of this faith now, we govern by tenderness. It is a tenderness which, long since cut off from the person of Christ, is wrapped in theory. When tenderness is detached from the source of tenderness, its logical outcome is terror."[2] According to O'Connor, all of our tenderness, when removed from the incarnation and the passion of Christ, will be abstract and thus able to justify any violence for the end of "tenderness." She intimates that such theoretical love of others will open the door to holocausts, genocides, or—in Oona's case—mercy killing.

O'Connor credits the character of Ivan Karamazov, from Dostoevsky's *The Brothers Karamazov*, with beginning this philosophy, that of discrediting God's goodness and thus disconnecting goodness from God. She intended to spend the summer of 1963 rereading Dostoevsky, so it is likely that his ideas influence episodes in the manuscript. The scene between the mother and daughter in particular shares resonance with Ivan's dialogue with his little demon.[3] Both pairs debate whether one can "love humanity" without loving those closest to you, those who are guilty, and those who are inconvenient. The devil delivers a speech mocking Ivan's ideas: "Love will be sufficient only for a moment of life, but the very consciousness of its momentariness will intensify its fire, which now is dissipated in dreams of eternal love beyond the grave."[4] Although the thoughts are what the young scholar Ivan had previously published in an article, hearing them from the mouth of his hallucination infuriates him.

Ivan calls the demon the worst part of himself. In the conversations between Oona and her mother, the two sound like halves of the same self, a Jekyll and Hyde pairing. Even after her mother has died, Oona hears her mother's voice echoing in her mind, criticizing her choices. Twenty-first-century readers may also hear in the mother-daughter dialogue unintended echoes of Alfred Hitchcock's *Psycho*—the "mother [who] wouldn't hurt a fly" but who possesses the serial killer Norman Bates. Or Chuck Palahniuk's *Fight Club*, in which the unnamed protagonist befriends the enigmatic Tyler Durden, who readers later discover is the narrator's hallucination. Together, the innocent party and his violent counterpart blow up a skyscraper. Like these psychotic renditions that come decades later, Oona and her mother are two sides of a coin. While the mother taught her daughter theories about how to live, she is affronted that her daughter intends to carry out their extreme consequences.

In the manuscripts, O'Connor changes the identity of Walter's correspondent multiple times, from his aunt to his cousin to the stranger Oona Gibbs.[5] Likely, O'Connor began with the idea of the aunt when she was working with an Asbury-like Walter, an artist living in New York and suffering from an unnamed sickness. As she began to familiarize herself with Walter, the scholar who stayed in the South, O'Connor started to draw a different picture of his activist pen pal, one unrelated to Walter and an outsider to Southern manners. The introduction to the aunt happens by chance as Walter attends the lecture on Vedanta, the same one that Asbury's roommate Goetz paid for him to attend in "The Enduring Chill." Instead of his eyes alighting on the priest in the crowd, Walter notices his aunt and her daughter.

Why Do the Heathen Rage?

WALTER'S AUNT[1]

The lecture on Vedanta had been a waste of his money as far as the lecture was concerned. While Goetz had listened enthralled to the dark little man on the platform, Walter, who was on the end of the horse-shoe shaped row, had let his bored gaze pass across the faces of several dark girls in saris, past a Japanese youth and several girls who looked like secretaries. Then toward the middle of the row, it had rested on a lean spectacled figure in black, a priest. Walter's attitude toward the priest was ambivalent. He had never met one, but he thought of them as having professional interest in death. The priest's expression was of a polite but strictly reserved interest and Walter identified his own feelings immediately, then he let his gaze travel on.

It traveled across several Jewish student faces and then stopped abruptly on a plump middle-aged woman with black hair, cut in the latest silly Italian fashion. His eyes remained on her in an open, blatant, shocked stare. Her face was his mother's face, vulgarized and disguised with high black arched eyebrows and an exaggerated red bowed mouth. His revulsion was sudden and intense. He uttered a sharp involuntary cry. Several faces turned toward him. He could not remove his eyes from the woman's face, even when she turned and looked at him. She gave him a cool instant of attention, then turned her head back to the speaker, her chin tilted just slightly higher as if she took his stare for the admiration to which she was accustomed.

Walter's heart thumped once like a ponderous leaden bell-slapper, flat and harsh. Who she was was as plain to him as if the revelation had been made by an invisible hand, writing on the white wall over her head: This is your aunt, your idol. Ponder. Ponder. Ponder.

She was listening with apparent intenseness to the speaker. Her eyes were narrowed but they shone with a hard, brilliant innocence. She had left Meadow Oaks thirty years before for all the right reasons, for all the same ones he had left. Everything she had done since had been admirable. She had never written a letter back, but she had not forgotten them. Every article she had ever had published, she had sent back home, anything that would infuriate her brother-in-law or disgust her sister or instruct her niece and nephew; and she had instructed them. If he and his sister had ever agreed on anything, it was only that their aunt, for her generation, had the family brains, the family conscience, the family—they gloried in the word—guts. She scorned manners, she scorned marriage, she scorned the dear old dirty Southland, and what she scorned she spit upon. They had fished her articles out of the waste-basket or rescued them on the way to the trash-burner. She had lived all over the world, in Paris and in Athens and in Singapore. She had lived.

She turned her head and looked at him again and this time he shifted his eyes. Of course, it could not be she. He would not look again. In a second his eyes were on her and they remained on her for the rest of the lecture, even when she looked at him again. Next to her sat a pale young girl, very plain, with a long, pinched nose and a lower jaw that hung slightly slack as if she were asthmatic or stupid or both. The girl sat with her arm on the older woman's chair and from time to time she let her head rest on the other's shoulder.

There is no satisfactory ending to these episodes because the story never begins. Other than in his dreams—where Walter and Oona are driving in a convertible with a group of "Negroes" toward the beach—Oona and Walter never meet.

I imagine Oona driving up to Walter's home the way someone may approach Andalusia. The trees bow over the intersec-
tion between the road and the highway, obscuring the entrance
to the farm. You feel as though you are driving beneath a scraggy
veil, watching it lift as the branches scrape your windshield. In
a convertible, Oona would have to duck the assaulting foliage.
The red dirt road to Andalusia is lined by trees right and left,
but there is no sign of a meadow or any conspicuously large
oaks. But Meadow Oaks would emerge before Oona as a long,
wide stretch of grass dotted with purple and yellow wildflow-
ers, with four monstrous trees standing like sentinels in the
middle. To her right would be an old white house perched on
a low hill. When Oona pulls up, it would not yet be noon, and
three people would be lounging on the porch.

Can you imagine how Oona would focus on Roosevelt, calling him "Walter" and anxious that he respond to her with affection? But her plastered smile would quickly thin as she realizes
the trick that has been played on her. We can feel for Roosevelt
in this scene. Tilman would have to wake the man from his
slumber in the rocking chair, likely with a knock of his cane
to Roosevelt's gut. As Roosevelt stirs, he would not be able to
comprehend what is happening, having no knowledge of the
game that Walter has been playing with his identity.

Then Walter appears, thudding down the stairs of his home
and throwing open the screen door. Before Oona's gaze, he
would look like a balding young man, wearing a blue shirt wrin-
kled and misbuttoned, his khaki trousers still torn from crossing
the barbed wire to take pictures of Boatright's shack, and he'd
be in the threadbare moccasins that disgust his mother and
that are so similar to the ones O'Connor herself wore. On the
bridge of his nose would sit pink, round spectacles.

Oona would not match Walter's fantasy of her either. From
O'Connor's descriptions, her hair was not long, not blond,
and not curled, though it may have been before her ride in the

convertible. She does not have full, voluptuous lips, but rather thin, parched ones. Her eyes are a vibrant green, but they appear vicious, like a feral cat's, and her nose is pinched in the middle. She would wear a handmade dress in a floral pattern that hung nearly to her ankles, as so many Greenwich Village bohemians did in the 1960s. The sleeves would be short so that people could see her arms, which may be covered with small freckles. Only her cheeks appear plump, like a child's, while the rest of her is thin, her skin drawn too tightly over her bones.

What would happen when these two meet? How would the raging heathens receive their comeuppance? How would Walter or Oona be transformed?

At the end of her life, Flannery worried over her powers to write the story she wanted to tell. She feared becoming a caricature of herself. In the manuscript, Walter thinks of his family:

> They were cartoons, too grotesque to belong even in Southern fiction. If Walter tried to put them into a story, their mere presence would turn it into a farce.[2]

Perhaps these thoughts reflect O'Connor's concerns about *Why Do the Heathen Rage?* Perhaps she feared that she was not writing these characters with the vitality that she wanted for them.

Readers who are familiar with O'Connor sometimes cast her stories as formulaic. Scholar Sarah Gordon writes, "O'Connor's stories may appear to follow a similar pattern. Indeed, when many of these stories are reduced to brief plot summaries, the reader understands a certain predictable unpredictability, or unpredictable predictability."[3] To write an O'Connor story, you need a character with a physical disability, a prideful Southern Protestant with a chip on their shoulder about God, and some violent catastrophe that humbles the protagonist into seeing a vision. There are exceptions to the rule, but, for the most part, O'Connor's stories—*after* being read and studied—can become predictable. But O'Connor appears to be wanting to write a different story in *Why Do the Heathen Rage?* These two characters could have fallen in love or killed each other; either of them could be converted and redeemed. Instead, because of O'Connor's premature death, Walter and Oona remain forever miles apart.

BURNING CROSSES

In 1948 a cross was burned on the home lawn of the president of Georgia State College for Women in Milledgeville, mere minutes from O'Connor's farm. The story made the front page of the *Atlanta Constitution*. The report reads, "A cross approximately 5-feet high was found blazing at the southeast entrance of the old Governor's Mansion. . . . The cross was discovered by 3 young women students. . . . Appearance of the fiery cross came on the heels of last week's incidents during a meeting of educators."[1] The previous week's "incidents" alludes to a meeting held on the college campus that included one hundred college presidents and deans, two of whom were Black. The educational conference had been threatened by the Ku Klux Klan, and the cross burning cut the event short. No Black administrator was willing to stay in Milledgeville after that. Little more than a week prior, Isaiah Nixon had been murdered in front of his whole family—because he had voted. His killers were later charged but freed by an all-white jury.

Almost a decade after the incident—as the danger for Black citizens in Milledgeville had grown—Flannery relates the 1948 cross burning to Maryat Lee. When visiting her brother, then president of Georgia State College for Women (1956–1967), Lee had accepted a ride home from Emmet, a Black farmworker. This seemingly innocuous act could have had violent consequences for Emmet or Lee. However, Lee seems undeterred by Flannery's caution, as she responds:

I am fascinated with my brush with dangerous forces. And have tried to imagine what my brother would do if he woke up with a firey [*sic*] cross in the camellia garden one night. Would he go out and attach the hose to the faucet and put it out? Or begin to pray? Or call the fire department? Or act as if it weren't there and ignore it like a gentleman—making sure first that it wouldn't burn up the trees or garage first?[2]

The idea of a burning cross becomes a joke between Flannery and Maryat, yet Flannery tries to attend seriously to Maryat's questions. She attempts to insert a cross-burning scene into her then novel-in-progress *The Violent Bear It Away*. As the episode plays out, the young Tarwater—who is named Thomas at this point in the drafts—is tempted to pray. John Rayber Sr. is the college president, delighted that the Ku Klux Klan have noticed him enough to put a cross in his yard.

The Violent Bear It Away

THE BURNT CROSS [1]

Thomas found it and stood for a long time staring at it as if he were not certain what he was looking at. It was two flat planks nailed together to form a cross, the vertical one about four feet, the other about three. It was stuck up exactly on the highest point of the rock garden. . . . Thomas stood for a long time staring at the cross, then he began to look around him at the empty windows of the buildings.

It was six-thirty in the morning and no one got up so early but him. He looked behind him across the lawn to the sidewalk and the street and the porches of the white houses. Nothing was stirring except a row of starlings that sat muttering hoarsely on the telephone wire that crossed the lawn. Thomas suddenly knelt down, and very red in the face, muttered, "rest in peace," three times.

After a minute a grey car drove up and two men got out of it and joined the other two around the cross. The four of them stood there with their hands behind them. John Rayber Junior was leaning as far away from him to hear. The side door of the president's house banged and his wife started down the steps, talking in her high nasal voice. The two trustees took off their hats when they saw her coming and then didn't look at her again. John Rayber Junior's father didn't take off his hat; his neck was craned forward as if he couldn't get enough of the cross and his mouth was stretched in a loose smile. His face looked as if he were alone in the bath tub, letting his thoughts float. She stood a little off from the four of them and kept on talking. The morning was damp and heavy; masses of yellow-green hid the fronts of the houses and the sky was the same color as the pavement. The ugly little cross looked like some scarecrow dwarf that had been burned to the bone in his tracks. John Rayber [the president] saw it silent and aflame, dropping out of the black sky and into the dark wet trees and now down, put out, onto the black wet grass.

"Do you know what the cross there means?"

Thomas scowled. "It means Jesus Christ was crucified," he said. "What do you take me for? An ass?"

Mr. Rayber allowed the smile to settle in one corner of his mouth. "Thomas," he said, at length, "it means a good deal more than that," and he turned and went into the house, erect and barefooted.

Why Do the Heathen Rage?

ONE POTENTIAL ENDING

What does the burning cross mean? For Flannery, like the young Thomas character in her drafts, the cross meant Jesus Christ crucified. For President John Rayber, it means a badge of honor: he has been deemed worthy of attention, even if it is public condemnation. However, neither of the white men in this scene register the horror behind that burning cross. In *The Cross and the Lynching Tree*, James Cone defines the cross in terms of its misuse by white supremacists: "The cross and the lynching tree are separated by nearly 2,000 years. One is the universal symbol of Christian faith; the other is the quintessential symbol of black oppression in America. Though both are symbols of death, one represents a message of hope and salvation, while the other signifies the negation of that message by white supremacy."[1] In the book of Acts, Jesus is described as "hanged on a tree" (5:30 KJV), an image that baptized the imagination of the African American community, uplifting their suffering to participation in Christ. The poet Countee Cullen uses this image in his poem "The Black Christ," which describes Jesus as "but the first leaf in a line / Of trees on which a Man should swing."[2] Cone documents historically how the cross, for African

Americans, not merely became conflated with the reality of the lynching tree but offered hope beyond it.

O'Connor understood the symbol of the cross, but she did not grasp the violence and oppression associated with the burning cross—that of the lynching tree. From her privileged place within her white world, O'Connor experienced no fear or repulsion when she read the news stories of burned crosses because she did not consider the implications of murder in the symbol, especially the threat to Black lives. When O'Connor saw those burning crosses, she thought of the uneducated rednecks who had no more sense than to make statements about their ignorance publicly. Men who supposedly worshiped Jesus each Sunday, where crosses adorned their churches' roofs, then burned those similar wooden beams on hillsides to showcase their hate. But O'Connor never connects the burning cross with the lynched bodies of African Americans. If only O'Connor had meditated on how those burning crosses terrorized her Black neighbors.

Although the cross-burning episode occurs in the manuscripts of O'Connor's second novel, I kept wanting to include it somehow in *Why Do the Heathen Rage?* I was unsatisfied with Walter's conversion, even as the starting point of the story, even for a secular contemplative who is intended to hear God's voice in a thin whisper. It was not simply because I was used to another type of Flannery story—the one with the intrusive presence of God and the Christ who haunts characters from behind trees—it was because Walter needed a slap in the face to change. He had to see that what he was doing was wrong, that by impersonating a Black person, he was not only lying, he was reducing people like Roosevelt to types, to caricatures, to Other. When I read the attempt to write of a burnt cross in *The Violent Bear It Away* manuscripts, I thought I had found a stronger impetus for transformation in Walter. Surely, a burning cross would be enough to scandalize the white intellectual and compel him to see the image of God not only in Oona but also in Eustis, Alice, and Roosevelt.

So I borrowed the material and played with it, trying to incorporate the burning of a cross into the *Why Do the Heathen Rage?* story. Borrowing lines from O'Connor's unfinished manuscripts—both *The Violent Bear It Away* and *Why Do the Heathen Rage?*—I filled in parts of the story, compiling a concluding scene for Walter, a moment of grace, as O'Connor always sought to offer her characters. Readers might find such an attempt at imitation presumptuous. "Yes, of course it is presumptuous," writes poet and scholar Angela Alaimo O'Donnell. In *Andalusian Hours*, O'Donnell adopts Flannery's voice and perspective as she writes 101 sonnets that tell O'Connor's biography. The poet defends her choice: "It is impossible to put oneself in the place of another human being, to imagine seeing the world through his or her eyes, and to clothe those thoughts with language without presuming."[3] All acts of imagination are presumptuous.

Any work that brings O'Connor's unfinished ideas before readers will be presumptuous. As editor Michael Pietsch wrote of David Foster Wallace's posthumous novel *The Pale King*, "Everyone who worked with David knows well how he resisted letting the world see work that was not refined to his exacting standard. But an unfinished novel is what we have, and how can we not look? David, alas, isn't here to stop us from reading or to forgive us for wanting to."[4] So, too, with this unfinished manuscript of Flannery O'Connor. We know little of her hopes and aspirations for this work; even less can we step into her shoes and revise it as she would have preferred. No one can be Flannery O'Connor; we can only presume.

A Presumptuous Attempt to End the Novel

It was six-thirty the next morning when Walter got up. He never rose early, but he had had a dream the night before and was still shaken. Walter seemed to be at a camp. There was a rock pool, and he was fourth in a line of sheet-draped boys who had become convinced that baptism was necessary for salvation. Seeing from his own eyes and outside of himself, Walter thought the boys looked around thirteen years old. Walter had rubber plugs in his ears. The first three went down nervously grinning into the water and came up, each with a hideous little silent gasp as if beneath the water there had been a vision of reality none was prepared for. The thought of bolting flashed as a large dark-skinned man, who must have been a preacher, grasped Walter and threw him backward with vicious unexpected strength into the crystal-clear water where a thousand microcosmic suns bounced. Walter felt nothing but the man's unwanted hands gripping him by the arms. From under the water, he gazed up into the man's brown eyes. The water obscured the man's image, so his face looked like an impressionist painting. Walter thought he was drowning, dying under the man's firm grip, when suddenly he was lifted out from under the pool, and he too let out a gasp. He was alive. When he woke up, he was clutching his bedsheet.

No one else seemed to be awake. The house was silent. From his window, Walter could see a row of starlings muttering hoarsely on an oak branch. Across the highway in the distance, on the hill of Boatright's property, there appeared a large, dark, looming figure, like the preacher from his dreams, only much thinner. The shape was so far off he couldn't make out exactly what it was.

Walter tiptoed downstairs and snuck quietly from the house. He started walking across the lawn between the properties, through the grass toward the object, drawn to it, the way he had been attracted to Oona or pulled by the man from his dream. As he passed the circle of oaks, they seemed to accompany him on his pilgrimage, like invisible soldiers gathering in his ranks, pressing him onward. He started to run without knowing what he was doing or why. The shape grew larger and more distinct the closer he came. Walter nearly leapt over the wire fence that he had tripped over the day before. He possessed an energy that did not seem to belong to him as he sprinted across the highway, past the objectionable shack, and quickly up the hill where the figure stood looming.

When Walter arrived at the top, he was panting, clutching his side. He thought his ribs might explode from within. His heart burned, and he bent over to catch his breath as his hands dropped from his side to his knees. Walter wiped his face with the tail of his shirt. The figure he had viewed from his window was two charred sticks crossed. The morning was damp and heavy. The ugly little cross looked like some scarecrow dwarf that had been burned to the bone in his tracks. Walter imagined it silent and aflame, dropping out of the sky and into the dark wet trees and now down, put out, on the wet grass. Part of him wanted to kneel before it or cross himself. "Rest in peace," entered his mind. He pushed these thoughts out and studied the charred sticks more closely.

An obnoxious whistle from behind startled him. Custer Boatright was lumbering up the hill, hoisting his pants with each step.

"Woo wee, what have we got here?" He winked at Walter, who looked away. The gesture made Walter feel guilty, as though Boatright were trying to share a secret with him. The fat man was smiling unpleasantly.

Both men continued staring ahead at the blackened cross before them. The sky seemed as blanched as dawn, as though the earth were no longer moving. Boatright placed his red, rock-like hand silently on Walter's shoulder. It remained there a moment, heavy and foreign and demanding.

"Well now, Walter, do you know what that there cross means?" Walter thought of a painting he had once seen of the crucifixion done by a German Renaissance artist. The dead man had been covered by sores because the painting had been put in a hospital where the patients suffered from a similar illness.

"It means Jesus Christ was crucified." Walter scowled. "I'm not an ass."

Boatright's smile settled into the corner of his mouth. "It means a good deal more than that."

Walter wrenched himself free from Boatright's hand. He ran from the hill as if chased by Satan. He descended down the hill as quickly as he had risen, his mind racing. As he darted across the pasture, he tripped over a rock and was sent flying through the air. When he landed, his face hit the ground hard. The wind was knocked out of him. Walter rested there a moment to collect his wits. The soil coated his sweat-doused skin and clung to him. His spectacles had broken in the fall, so he tucked the pieces into his shirt pocket and began to walk home.

Through his blurred vision, the four oaks towered, looking more like primal monsters than old trees. He traced a path toward home slowly, unsure of every step. His eyes saw everything before him as through a veil, yet he also saw better than ever. Like Paul, he had been thrown to the ground and blinded, but his will was out of kilter.

When Walter had read Oona's first letter, he had recognized her theological error. It had been necessary that his system ward off the full force of the discovery he had made, but his logical mind was already sorting out the consequences. If Oona had abrogated the place of God, then he believed in God. Walter had not up until that moment been a believer. But he realized then, with a jolt, that he was. He was a Christian, bound for hell. Walter knew the Fathers of the Church, he had assisted at Nicaea and at Chalcedon. He had explored the intricacies of Light with Bonaventure; he knew where Aquinas and Duns Scotus would part company. He had seen the path turn downward with Abelard and illogic enter, grandly eloquent, with Luther. He had been active at Trent. He had adhered always to the most orthodox line but never once, never for the slightest moment, had it occurred to him, even remotely, to believe any of it; or that there was the least danger of his doing so. Only now it simply appeared the accomplished truth. Grace originated elsewhere and grace was. It mattered and worse, Oona mattered.

As Walter walked through the front door, he ignored the wasps building a nest above the frame. He closed the door on them without ducking, having no fear of being stung. In a trance, his eyes glazed over, Walter stalked upstairs to the washroom, not needing his glasses to see the way. Then he stood before the sink to clean his face and was taken aback by the image in the hanging mirror that stared at him. It was his face but not his face. Covered in black earth and distorted by his poor eyesight, his face resembled that of the man from his dream. Walter's heart began to thump. The face was bloody, severe, and black. It regarded him suspiciously. Under its gaze, Walter looked untrustworthy, ungracious, even evil. Walter shuddered.

As I watched Walter run toward that burnt cross—originally found on Rayber's porch—I knew he had to fall. He had to be like the eager servant in Julian of Norwich's *Revelations of Divine Love* whom the Lord allows to fall so that he can help him out of the ditch. Julian credits the mercy of God that grants the fallen one the grace to see his fall as a move toward the lowness and meekness that is needed to behold God.[5] The New Testament meaning of the Greek word *skandalon*, from which we draw our word "scandalize," is "stumbling block," that which causes one to fall. For O'Connor, the stumbling block from the Scriptures is the execution and resurrection of the incarnate God. As she writes in the "Author's Note" to the second edition of *Wise Blood*, "That belief in Christ is to some a matter of life and death has been a stumbling block for readers who would prefer to think it a matter of no great consequence."[6] Through her fiction, O'Connor moves readers to stumble and fall, to be brought to lowness and meekness, and to feel with Hazel Motes, with Tarwater, and with Walter that belief in Christ is a matter of life and death.

For O'Connor, this belief must be brought about by changed vision. In O'Connor's first novel *Wise Blood*, Hazel Motes burns his physical eyes to blindness in order to gain spiritual sight. In *The Violent Bear It Away*, Francis Marion Tarwater experiences a metaphorical burning. The narrator describes him with "singed eyes, black in their deep sockets" as they "envision the fate that awaited him."[7] Throughout her stories, O'Connor draws attention to characters' limited vision (consider the serial killer The Misfit, who wears glasses but has stronger spiritual sight than the grandmother), or she emphasizes a partial spiritual acuity (in "The Enduring Chill," the small-town priest Father Finn has "one fierce eye inflamed").[8]

We notice at the start of *Why Do the Heathen Rage?* that Tilman possesses one raging eye while Walter relies on his glasses. There's an episode where Tilman carves eyeglass frames out of wood for Roosevelt, a scene that O'Connor excised and included in her short story "Judgement Day." Who knows what O'Connor would have made of these motifs, but I tried to imitate moves that she makes in other stories by letting Walter fall and break his glasses. Perhaps hazy physical vision would move Walter toward truer spiritual sight.

In "Everything That Rises Must Converge," O'Connor draws readers' attention to mirrors as the medium for distorting vision, whereas icons offer a corrective. At the start of the story, the mother keeps staring at herself in the mirror, repeating what the saleslady told her about her new hat: "You won't see yourself coming and going." When the mother literally sees her image mirrored back in the Black mother who boards the bus and sits across from her wearing the same purple hat, she lacks the ability to see herself in the woman. In imitation of this scene, I attempted to modify O'Connor's unfinished baptism scene with Walter so that the preacher—whom I recast as a Black man— would become the icon that views Walter. Walter needed to see himself from outside himself, from the perspective of someone he was pretending to be, which is why I cast the preacher as a Black man. If Walter lost his glasses, perhaps the distorted image in the mirror would draw up the preacher's way of seeing Walter. Perhaps, like other O'Connor characters who receive revelation, Walter would see himself as another sees him.

"Did I tell you that the Ku Klux Klan met across the road Saturday night before last. They burned a cross—just for the sake of ceremony. We could have seen it out our upstairs windows but we didn't know until it was over. You ought to be down to observe mid-August politics in Georgia. You would return with curled hair," Flannery writes Maryat Lee on August 17, 1962.[9] It had been over a decade since the cross was burned on Georgia College's lawn and the sight, for O'Connor, was then closer to home. Did O'Connor fail to carry out a fictive encounter with a burning cross because of her position in the world of the South?

Two decades before O'Connor began writing her third novel, another white American novelist, Willa Cather, had tried to tackle the issue of race and failed. Her 1940 work *Sapphira and the Slave Girl* gives away its failure in the title: the slave girl has no name in the title. Throughout the story, the slave girl, Nancy, is a pawn in the game of Sapphira, a white woman who is struggling to overcome her anxiety about her disability and the way she fears it threatens the stability of her marriage. As Toni Morrison points out in *Playing in the Dark: Whiteness and the Literary Imagination*, "The problem is trying to come to terms critically and artistically with the novel's concerns: the power and license of a white slave mistress over her female slaves. How can that *content* be subsumed by some other meaning? How can the story of a white mistress be severed from a consideration of race and the violence entailed in the story's premise?"[10] The same problem confronts O'Connor without her knowing it: she is trying to write about race as one element of a story about the theological problems that face secular contemplatives and secular social activists. By not reading the issue of race with theological significance—which *must* include the Black perspective that so often eluded her—O'Connor seems to have been unable to finish the story she longed to tell.

THE OTHER HALF
OF THE STORY

On December 14, 1939, a ten-year-old boy has been dressed up as a slave to sing in a Black boys choir at a charity ball in Atlanta. Behind him is a mock-up of a Southern plantation and before him sits the cast from *Gone with the Wind*, including Vivien Leigh and Clark Gable, and the author of the novel, Margaret Mitchell. The next evening a hundred thousand eager Southerners will flood the streets outside the Loew's Grand Theatre to watch the group parade across the red carpet. Civil War veterans line up to shake the hands of Hollywood stars. Of its ten Academy Awards, one will go to Hattie McDaniel, the first African American to win an Oscar, yet she is noticeably missing from the prestigious premiere. None of the Black actors from the film were allowed to attend the event in Atlanta, despite the protest of the fellow cast members and the consternation of the producer David O. Selznick. Unbeknownst to him, the boy singing in the choir at this segregated event, in celebration of this film that romanticizes the antebellum South, will become the nation's number one civil rights hero. In the midst of this moment of racial tension, young Martin Luther King Jr. belts out a tune to the applause of an all-white room.

Only five miles north from downtown Atlanta,[1] fourteen-year-old Flannery O'Connor is turning up her nose at the unnecessary spectacle. *Gone with the Wind* and its sentimental nostalgia for a past that never existed will annoy O'Connor for the next few decades as she writes. In her story "A Late Encounter with the Enemy"—penned in 1952—she pokes fun at the impotent and delusional Civil War veteran George Poker Sash who is dressed up in a general's uniform for the premiere. For the rest of his life, he remembers nothing of the war itself but holds tightly to the memory of "that preemie they had in Atlanta."[2] Here, O'Connor associates memories of the Civil War with charades. They are a fantasy of the generation that calls itself the Old South.

While *Gone with the Wind* opens with a romantic description of the Old South as the "land of Cavalier and Cotton Fields," a "pretty world [where] Gallantry took its last bow," and speaks of this world as a "Civilization gone with the wind,"[3] the reality was that Irish immigrants and European convicts had migrated to the South, worked the land, and exploited slaves to build up pretentious homes. In his exposé *The Mind of the South*, W. J. Cash explains that property was the real distinction of class, not education, manners, or tradition. "Aristocracy in any real sense did not develop until after the passage of a hundred years—until after 1700. . . . The number of those who had moved the whole way into aristocracy even by the time of the Revolution was small."[4] Most of these property holders were still illiterate, and life in the South still rough and crude. The myth of aristocracy was precisely that—a fictitious story about their history and noble beginnings. Cash asks, Was the ruling class of the great South "anything, for the great part, but the natural flower of the backcountry grown prosperous?"[5] Economic success masqueraded as providential and noble inheritance. None of it fooled Flannery for a second.

When Milledgeville celebrated the centennial of the Civil War, Flannery went into town for the public opening of the Cline Mansion. Built in 1820, the mansion had served as residence for the governor in 1838–1839, and O'Connor herself had lived there with aunts and cousins at intervals throughout her life. But such pomp held no sway over O'Connor's imagination. Although she, like Mitchell, had learned her history from Civil War veterans, she knew that the South had been defeated. Unlike Mitchell, a Georgia reactionary, O'Connor thought the fall was for the best. As she tells her friend Louise Abbot in January 1961, "I sure am sick of the Civil War."[6]

For those of us in the twenty-first century, the Civil War feels as distant in the past as the American Revolution; yet during O'Connor's lifetime, veterans still swung on porches and told stories of their heroic fight against the villainous North. When O'Connor was being educated, she had to steel her mind against two generations of adults who believed in the nobility of the Lost Cause, who celebrated films like *Gone with the Wind* with fanfare, and who harped on her for not writing a similar bestseller. As the mother in "The Enduring Chill" advises her artist son, "We need another good book like *Gone with the Wind*. . . . Put the war in it. . . . That always makes a good long book."[7] One can imagine how countercultural the young Flannery must have appeared in her aspirations to write more honest fiction.

When O'Connor talks of the Civil War, she does not romanticize the South's loss but theologizes it. Walker Percy, responding to a reporter who had asked why there were so many good Southern writers, said, "Because we lost the War."[8] O'Connor explains this quip: "He didn't mean by that simply that a lost war makes good subject matter. What he was saying was that we have had our Fall."[9] In other words, O'Connor reads the South as a community that acknowledges human limitation. Unlike the North, which strives for progress and visualizes a future utopia brought about by consumerism and industry, the South has its feet grounded by defeat.

The inward knowledge of defeat should lead to humility. O'Connor's characters are brought down from their high places. She does not broker with Civil War fantasies, because they lie

about the past. It is the truth that she is after. When writing
about the fiction writer and his country—and by "country" she
means place, not nation—O'Connor says:

> To know oneself is to know one's region. It is also to know the
> world, and it is also, paradoxically a form of exile from that
> world. The writer's value is lost, both to himself and to his
> country, as soon as he ceases to see that country as a part of
> himself, and to know oneself is, above all, to know what one
> lacks. It is to measure oneself against the Truth, and not the
> other way around.[10]

A novelist disconnected from truth, as Margaret Mitchell appears to be, tells a story according to how she wants to see the
world, not according to the way the world *is*. Mitchell's fantasy
about the South, its victimization at the hands of the North
and her whitewashed portrayal of slavery, perpetuates pride.
For O'Connor, the writer must submit to truth and be judged
by it. From the stance of limitation, the writer will tell a more
honest story, one that hopefully leads to both her own and her
readers' humility. O'Connor wants to tell the true story, but,
as other writers have pointed out, she was missing an essential
part of the story.

In 1974, a decade after O'Connor died, Alice Walker visited
O'Connor's home outside Milledgeville. Before Walker knocks
on the door of the white house at Andalusia farm, she and her
mother lunch at a "garish new Holiday Inn" across the highway. They discuss O'Connor, integration, corn muffins, and
peacocks. Walker explains to her mother why she undertakes
these pilgrimages South to authors' homes. She laments that
"history [is] split up, literature split up, and people are split
up too. It makes people do ignorant things."[11] As an example,
Walker relates to her mother a story about when she presented
at a gathering of Mississippi librarians. Before she began to
speak, one of the listeners stood up and said that she "really
did think Southerners wrote so well because 'we' lost the war."

The words of Percy and O'Connor sound hollow when Walker repeats them, for "we" refers only to the *white* Southerners. Walker adds a correction that Percy and O'Connor missed. "'We' didn't lose the war," Walker responds. "'You all' lost the war. And you all's loss was our gain."[12]

When I first started reading the *Why Do the Heathen Rage?* manuscripts, I found nothing odd about the fact that O'Connor had not finished her novel. After all, she had taken years to write the previous ones. Novels were not her primary genre; she wrote stronger short stories. She was also very sick over the last few years of her life and did not have the energy to work on such a long piece. I made all sorts of excuses for O'Connor's inability to complete the novel. Other scholars had noted that O'Connor was moving in a new direction—starting with a conversion rather than leading up to it and creating a Catholic contemplative protagonist instead of a fundamentalist prophet.[13] These explanations all work, but there seemed to be a big gap we were all failing to see.

Only Virginia Wray, who writes in 1994 about O'Connor's shortcomings with this unfinished novel, seemed to catch a glimmer of why O'Connor struggled to complete it. She notes that the "larger things" with which O'Connor was grappling were "likely issues of social justice and fairness."[14] It was Wray's dismissive tone toward eternal things (*sub specie aeternitatis*) that bothered me and prevented me from reading her argument well. The eternal things are the subject matter of O'Connor's work, and Wray assumes that O'Connor hides under eternal considerations for fear of dealing with the present. Wray writes, "Just as O'Connor was unable to reconcile her intellectual understanding of the need for social activism in the 1950s and 1960s with her own frequent retreat to the perspective of *sub specie aeternitatis*, so she was unable to focus and complete a third novel with two main characters illustrative of these polarized perspectives."[15] I questioned the word "retreat." O'Connor never retreated, and when it came to eternal things, for O'Connor, there was nothing higher or larger.

O'Connor was in the process of unearthing the eternal from the social chaos of the present. In a prayer she scribbled in her journal as a master's student in Iowa, she asks God, "Please help me get down under things and find where you are."[16] While social activism is necessary in the present, O'Connor wanted to dig below the surface of the contemporary events to see the invisible workings of providence. All of her fiction tries to exist in this universal vein, which requires prophetic vision. In her essay on Catholic novelists, she describes the prophetic vision not as that which predicts the future but as that which "is good for all time," a realism "of distances," of seeing the hoped-for apocalypse closer up.[17] Prophetic vision does not depict the facts of the moment so much as portray the mystery of the human hearts participating in the events.

Theologian Walter Brueggemann published a book entitled *The Prophetic Imagination* in 1978 and years later heard that this phrase had been used to describe O'Connor's imagination. In the foreword of the second edition of his book, Brueggemann explains what he means by "prophetic imagination": "an artistic direction in which truth is told in a way and at an angle that assures it will not be readily coopted or domesticated by hegemonic interpretive power."[18] The "angle" protects mystery from becoming an agenda, story from becoming didacticism. As O'Connor explains, "It is the realism which does not hesitate to distort appearances in order to show a hidden truth."[19] An artist must distort the surface level to show the roots where God is. Her character The Misfit claims that Jesus done "thrown everything off balance."[20] Because we walk around in our circumstances without recognizing that imbalance, O'Connor must destabilize our vision so we can see what needs correction.

For Brueggemann, the biblical prophets impel us to adopt a subversive vision of the world by inhabiting a prophetic imagination, first absorbing the Scriptures that throw everything off balance and then embodying such an imagination in how we interact with the skewed world. He italicizes his thesis: "*The task of prophetic ministry is to nurture, nourish, and evoke a consciousness and perception alternative to the consciousness and perception of the dominant culture around us.*"[21] That dominant culture is characterized by fast-paced responses, consumerism, utilitarianism, dehumanizing transactional relationships with people and the earth; it is a royal consciousness in which people live for their individual desires and material success. The prophetic imagination offers an alternative vision of the world, one rooted in an experience of suffering, loss, and exile but with a hope of healing, reconciliation, and home.

O'Connor writes from this prophetic imagination and against the royal consciousness in her fiction. Her offensively titled short story "The Artificial N——" is a great example. The story centers on a white man, Mr. Head, and his ten-year-old grandson Nelson. Toni Morrison reads the opening of the story where Mr. Head is cast as a king: the moon seems to request his "permission to enter" and even his trousers hang as though "flung to his servant" on the back of a chair, having a "noble air" as though "awaiting an order."[22] In O'Connor's fiction, readers see indirectly through the character's eyes, but they see also with some distance provided by the omniscient narrator. This double vision provides a gap between the two ways of seeing, so that readers can assess whether Mr. Head is as kingly as he imagines himself to be.

The story is titled thus so that readers who use such slandering language will be invited to read the story. O'Connor has written for a white readership, and for a specific type of white reader—one who feels no discomfort with the N-word. However, the story is meant to disabuse these readers of their prejudice; as the title foreshadows, the N-word represents an "artificial" construct. In the story, Mr. Head—an obvious allusion to his proud ego—teaches his grandson not to see human beings but to see skin color and to label people accordingly with this derogatory term. In contrast to Mr. Head's use of the N-word, the narrator writes only "Negro," the socially accepted reference of that time. The gap between the two visions provides the "angle" that Brueggemann speaks of, the place where mystery, to use O'Connor's preferred word, resides—where readers experience an alternative consciousness separate from the dominant narrative.

Although Mr. Head intends to instill racism in his grandson Nelson, the lesson is undone by Mr. Head's denial of the boy. Trying to teach the boy a lesson, Mr. Head hides from Nelson until the boy—fearful and frantic—runs into a woman and causes her to break her ankle. Mr. Head is so embarrassed that he denies knowing the boy. Those around him are "repulsed by a man who would deny his own image and likeness."[23] Because Mr. Head has placed himself at the center of his universe, even Nelson has become Other to him. The language alludes to Genesis 1:27, in which God creates human beings "in his own image and likeness." O'Connor shows how the process of othering strangers leads to the severance of even those most alike. She is trying to undo, not reinforce, Otherness.

The climactic moment of grace occurs when the two stumble upon the statue of a Black figure eating a slice of brown watermelon. Notably, the statue is missing one eye. Again invoking O'Connor's use of double vision in her fiction, the blindness in one eye or enlargement of one eye indicates a greater deference to spiritual over material vision or vice versa. She explains the choice to a friend: "What I had in mind to suggest with the artificial n—— was the redemptive quality of the Negro's suffering for us all."[24] Without the option of centering a Black Jesus in the story, O'Connor describes this statuette as being as close to one as possible. The two characters imitate the pose of the statue and thus mirror one another; their differences dissolve before the figure "like an action of mercy."[25] This Black icon has judged them both by his figuring of suffering, caused by their complicity in racism, and they are filled with shame. As they leave the statue, its judgment remains with them, and Mr. Head feels the mercy that has covered "his pride like a flame and consumed it."[26]

While O'Connor intended the ending of the story to be revelatory—for Mr. Head, of course, but even more for the reader—the conclusion has been problematized. Morrison, an adept and insightful reader of O'Connor's work, reads the epiphanic moment as a rescue for Mr. Head and Nelson from becoming strangers in the city. Seeing "a visual connection to what they believe is a shared racism of all whites of all classes," Mr. Head and Nelson are united against the Black Other.[27] Morrison argues, "The education of the boy is complete: he has been successfully and artfully taught racism and believes he has acquired respectability, status. And the illusion of power through the process of inventing an Other."[28] For Morrison, the statue of the Black jockey has no other role than as an emblem of racism, and thus the two may return home feeling racially superior.

Reflecting on the experience of his grandparents who, as children, were chided and assaulted by white children, Clint Smith underlines how racism has to be taught to be passed down, as it is in "The Artificial N——." Smith writes, "These children were not born to hate this way. They had been taught. They had watched their parents and they had watched the world and this is what they had been shown."[29] What Smith has observed in the stories of his grandparents, O'Connor depicts in her story: racism is not innate but purposefully handed down. O'Connor's story suggests that we may then be responsible for changing that—we can pass down anti-racism instead.

However, O'Connor's story fails to persuade Toni Morrison—a celebrated Black reader and fellow Catholic—of its prophetic vision. While Morrison appreciates O'Connor's "honesty and profound perception [of] the stranger, the outcast, Other," she holds the story up as an example "of how and why blacks are so vital to a white definition of humanity."[30] O'Connor's prophetic imagination failed to see the connection between royal consciousness—as delineated by Brueggemann—and white privilege. While she practiced a prophetic imagination, speaking out against the reigning consciousness in support of an eschatological vision, O'Connor was limited in her way of defining that empire.

When it came to race, which in itself was a false construct created by systems of power, O'Connor could not write about it persuasively for all readers. Margaret Earley Whitt, in her investigation into the significance of the civil rights movement for O'Connor's fiction, laments that O'Connor could not connect the civil rights message "to her own talent for fiction; she saw the palette from which she drew the colors of her universe not as the current events of social history but as the earlier events of biblical history. In the reality of the mid-twentieth century Milledgeville, she lived her life on one side of a parallel universe—in the white world, not in the black."[31] O'Connor did not make the imaginative leap to seeing Black lives as part of the alternative consciousness, to connecting Black bodies with their theological significance in the Christian imagination.

For O'Connor, the civil rights movement was an earthly and political issue, and thus it invited little investigation into its heavenly importance. While she would never accept the fallacy that eschatological justice excuses contemporary participation in correcting the wrongs of the moment, O'Connor had not been personally wounded by the sin of racism. Complicit, yes. Culturally guilty, yes. But O'Connor may not have heard from any friends about their sufferings; she may not have received

the news about the numerous lynchings and murders through-
out her state. Without feeling the damage caused by racism,
O'Connor perhaps felt no compulsion toward repentance.
Though we should be wary to judge her in hindsight.

We know that O'Connor needed time to reflect on contemporary events in order to transform them into fiction that spoke
to the deeper reality. For instance, the Montgomery bus boycott
took place during 1955–1956, but O'Connor does not write a
story about it until 1961, in "Everything That Rises Must Converge." In contrast, Eudora Welty quickly jotted down "Where
Is the Voice Coming From?" only weeks after the assassination
of NAACP leader Medgar Evers. O'Connor thought such cru-
sades made for bad fiction, for stories that skimmed the surface.
What O'Connor wanted to do was write eternal visions that
energized long-lasting action.

If we look at just the spring of 1963—when O'Connor was
deep into working on *Why Do the Heathen Rage?*—the country
saw an unprecedented number of demonstrations. According
to Justice Department records, there were more than 978 demonstrations in 109 cities, with over two thousand arrests and
four deaths that spring, including the assassination of Evers in
Jackson, Mississippi.[32] However, O'Connor would have needed
time to meditate on these events before they became part of the
story she could tell. O'Connor died as the movement was gain-
ing momentum. "Had she lived," Whitt wonders, "O'Connor
might have seen anew what her segregated world obscured."[33]

O'Connor mistrusted activism in general because of its association with posturing intellectuals. When she tried to write
about the 1953 murders that took place in Milledgeville in
"The Partridge Festival," written between 1959 and 1963 about
the killings by Marion Stembridge, she creates caricatures of
the main characters, two white intellectuals who uplift the

murderer as the victim and venture to prison to hear his story. As these characters reinterpret the murderer as an innocent scapegoat whose violence was a deserved recompense for a small-minded town, they quote impious clichés at one another and are frustrated that they sound like copies of each other's liberal leanings instead of autonomous free thinkers. O'Connor parodies the attempt at nonconformity as just conformity of another stamp.

While O'Connor greatly esteems some activists—such as her friend Father McCown—she explicitly disapproves of those who appear to have thoughtlessly joined the ranks. How O'Connor depicts Oona and how she writes about Mary Ann suggests that O'Connor believed that activism requires the cross at its core. O'Connor applauds Martin Luther King Jr. and Dorothy Day for acting as they did because they suffered alongside the poor, were willing to be arrested, and endured rebukes as they marched for equality. In O'Connor's eyes, King and Day were "doing what [one] can do and has to do."[34]

Yet O'Connor disapproved of her friend Maryat Lee's seeming sentimentalization of causes. Maryat Lee may have sounded too much like Ivan Karamazov or Albert Camus's hero, both of whom discredit the goodness of God because of suffering in the world. "In this popular pity, we mark our gain in sensibility and our loss in vision," O'Connor observes. "In the absence of this faith now, we govern by tenderness. It is a tenderness which, long since cut off from the person of Christ is wrapped in theory. When tenderness is detached from the source of tenderness, its logical outcome is terror. It ends in forced-labor camps and in the fumes of the gas chamber."[35] O'Connor claims that a tenderness without its roots in the deep place where God is, without its call to suffering, will lead to violence.

From O'Connor's stories, we see over and over again that we kill those whom we are meant to love the most. In "A Good Man Is Hard to Find," a serial killer shoots a grandmother who extends her hand in kindness toward him. In *The Violent Bear It Away*, a rebellious teen drowns his disabled cousin. In "The Comforts of Home," a frustrated homebody pulls the trigger and accidentally murders his mother. O'Connor warns us away from our penchant for violence by pointing the finger in our direction. Without this finger pointed in our direction, telling us that we are capable of such violence, people will keep dying. If we cannot even imagine that we are capable of this violence, then we are most prone to it. A 2015 icon created to honor those shot because of their skin color was titled *Our Lady, Mother of Ferguson and All Those Killed by Gun Violence*. The icon depicts Mary as a Black woman with her hands in a posture of surrender. Over her heart a silhouette of Jesus imitates her, posed in the crosshairs of an unseen gun. This image fits thematically with O'Connor's stories. They both warn us that the tallies will keep ticking if we do not choose to look through the statistics and see in others the face of Jesus Christ.

In her third novel, O'Connor turns to the issues of race and the civil rights movement but perhaps with too many blind spots, too many missing pieces, too little time to reflect on rather than parody her characters. O'Connor appears to write for white readers without imagining Black readers; in her letters, she considers the issue of rights only in civil terms and not according to theological necessities. When she writes of Black characters, O'Connor fails to envision their perspective and does not try to enter their minds—the protagonist Walter even grapples with a perceived lack of connection between himself as white and the African Americans around him. Most significantly, in depicting the motivations of an activist, O'Connor satirizes more than empathizes with Oona Gibbs.

However, "Was O'Connor a racist?" is a poor question to ask for at least two reasons: (1) to label a person is to reduce them and (2) we must not misconstrue the biographical person with the artwork. If human beings are in process, incomplete until death—and by Flannery's belief, still being purged in the afterlife—then an insult such as "racist" dismisses a person's humanity, their ability to grow and change. One of the reasons that people create art, debate publicly, become activists is because they believe that change is possible. Artists hope to alter the way that people see, removing planks from our eyes, opening us up to broader visions, allowing us to witness and empathize with a perspective that is not our own. People argue in the public square for similar reasons, to challenge their opponents' assumptions and correct errors. To label someone as racist or sexist, bigot or charlatan, and so on, is to deem that person incapable of change; they should be disinvited from the community.

Cancel culture functions on the premise that people may be reduced to the worst things they ever said or did. In 2020 when O'Connor biographer Paul Elie published an incendiary article titled "How Racist Was Flannery O'Connor?" he left no room for counterargument.[36] Although many of us tried to debate the issue and found the question itself dismissive, the damage had been done by the insinuation. If Flannery O'Connor said or did racist things, then she—and thus her work—needed to be canceled. That very week, students at Loyola University Maryland clamored to remove Flannery O'Connor's name from their dorm. Some of those who signed the online petition "didn't know that Flannery was a woman," nor had they read her fiction, essays, or letters.[37] Rather, they took Elie's word for it that she was racist, and Flannery's name was removed within the next month.

The major evidence for O'Connor's racism comes from her letters to Maryat Lee, which scholars have read as comic performance but which Elie finds "plainly sincere." Whether O'Connor was instigating her friend—as Walter does with Oona Gibbs—or whether she meant what she said ("I'm an integrationist by principle & a segregationist by taste anyway"), the worst of her statements should not allow readers to conflate biography with art. In *Breaking Bread with the Dead*, Alan Jacobs writes of the disparity between the intentions of our noble writers of the past and their ignoble deeds—mentioning by name Thomas Jefferson and John Milton. Rather than cancel these writers, Jacobs suggests, "We should not be surprised that they failed to live up to their ideals; we should, I think, be surprised that in their time and place they upheld such ideals at all. They pushed the world a little closer to freedom and justice. Of how many of us can that be said?"[38]

I'm of the ilk who does not excuse O'Connor's sins, nor do I cast the first stone. From my reading of her work, O'Connor was aiming at her principles in her art—integration—and fighting against her poor taste—the segregation of which she was accustomed by her region. It reminds me a bit of my husband who grew up in a complementarian church and could never imagine a woman preaching. When we were dating, he told me that theoretically he could get behind a woman preacher, but the sight and sound of it disturbed him. Now, a decade later, he would never say that. Unfortunately, O'Connor did not have a decade to be reconciled to integration; she died a month after the Civil Rights Act was signed. But her stories, like the writings of Jefferson and Milton, have moved me closer to knowing freedom and justice.

As a fiction writer, O'Connor knew her place was not making speeches on behalf of the rights of African Americans, but she was called to her typewriter to write stories. In a fall 1963 interview, O'Connor defends her choice: "The fiction writer is interested in individuals, not races; he knows that good and evil are not apportioned along racial lines and when he deals with topic matters, if he is any good, he sees the long run through the short run."[39] O'Connor lived through a time period when heathens assassinated saints—not that much has changed in the decades between her death and our reading of this manuscript.

Her problem was in trying to identify the difference between the two: Who are the heathens? Who are the saints? Her characters, like her readers, were both.

After a circuit of lectures in 1963, O'Connor returns to *Why Do the Heathen Rage?* but with frustration over its progress. She writes Cecil Dawkins of her concerns about the story: "My trouble right now is that I am beset by too many possibilities and can't make up my mind."[40] Seemingly dissatisfied with the options for her novel, O'Connor turns to a new story, "Revelation." Less than a month after expressing her concerns about the unfinished novel, O'Connor faints and never recovers entirely.

O'Connor's final published story, "Revelation," best concludes her intentions for eradicating racism from herself and readers.[41] Southern white woman Ruby Turpin is humiliated in a doctor's office by a college student named Mary Grace. Mrs. Turpin has been rattling on, expressing her disdain for those she considers beneath her: Blacks, white trash, and Mary Grace, who wears a sour expression on an unattractive face. In her interior thoughts, Mrs. Turpin thanks Jesus for "not [making] her a n—— or white-trash or ugly."[42] Overwhelmed with gratitude, she shouts aloud, "Thank you, Jesus, for making everything the way it is!" To which Mary Grace responds by throwing a book at Mrs. Turpin's eye, knocking her down, and attempting to strangle her. With eyes burning as they focus on Mrs. Turpin, Mary Grace whispers, "Go back to hell where you came from, you old wart hog!"[43]

The moment scandalizes Mrs. Turpin, and at the end of the story, she stands atop a fence above the pig pen on her farm and yells at God for answers. Although the insult came from a stranger's lips, the words have sunk in as though God has called her out. She questions the Lord, as she mindlessly does her chores, "How am I a hog and me both? How am I saved and from hell too?" O'Connor could aim the questions inward at herself: How can she be a sinner and a believer? How can she be racist and write such anti-racist stories? When Mrs. Turpin finally rages and roars, "Who do you think you are?" the question echoes back to her as though God is speaking: "Who do you think you are?" The proud woman must be knocked down to her rightful place, humble before the Lord.

As the sun sets, Mrs. Turpin receives a vision. A bridge extends from the earth "through a field of living fire." A congregation of souls who are "white-trash, . . . black n——s in white robes and battalions of freaks and lunatics" are dancing and leaping. One should recall King David's holy revelry before the ark of God, in which his wife thought he appeared foolish, but he was a man after God's own heart. Mrs. Turpin observes that those like herself and her husband Claud follow at the end of the line, for, as Jesus told his followers, the first shall be last and the last shall be first. The vision puts her in her place, so to speak, and she watches as even her so-called "virtues," her "dignity" and "common sense and respectable behavior" are "being burned away" by God's holiness. Following this revelation, Mrs. Turpin literally steps "down" from where she stands and descends the "slow way" back home.[44]

The summer of 1964, as O'Connor checked in to the hospital for the last time, she joked with Maryat Lee in a letter that she would sign her name "Mrs. Turpin."[45] This signature reveals so much about Flannery's view on racism and her own failings. Paul Elie mistakenly interprets this act as a sign that O'Connor embraced racism.[46] However, Mrs. Turpin is not lifted up in the story as a model to be followed; her faults are exposed and denounced. O'Connor writes in her essays that it is the duty of the Christian novelist to reflect the devil we are possessed by.[47] "Revelation" holds a mirror up even to the author. From this reflection, O'Connor sees herself possessed by racism and awaiting purgation. Writing the story reveals how much her fiction exorcised the worst of her sins.

When O'Connor began writing again in mid-January 1964, she focused on "Parker's Back" (extracting Gunnels from *Why Do the Heathen Rage?*) and revised a story from her MFA thesis, "The Geranium," into "Judgement Day." Although O'Connor continued to edit stories from her bed at Baldwin County Hospital, she admitted to spending more of her time reading than writing. By May, O'Connor relayed her fears that she would not have the energy to revise any of her stories for the new collection, which was published posthumously as *Everything That Rises Must Converge* (1965). The prospects of her hospital release began to look slimmer and slimmer, though in June she returned home for a spell. Unfortunately, the pain, the steroids, and the lack of energy compounded to keep O'Connor from working any further on her third novel. At the start of July, O'Connor called the priest to provide the Sacrament of the Sick, what once was known as Extreme Unction, the last sacrament of a dying Catholic.[48] She never again worked on *Why Do the Heathen Rage?*

Two years before O'Connor died, she made an interesting assertion in one of her essays that seems applicable to her final novel. "The story was as unfinished as the child's face," O'Connor writes, referring to the deformed visage of Mary Ann, a young girl who had lived and died in a cancer home in nearby Atlanta, and whose memory was preserved by nuns in *A Memoir of Mary Ann*, for which O'Connor composed the introduction. "Both seemed to have been left," O'Connor continues, "like the creation on the seventh day, to be finished by others. The reader would have to make something of the story as Mary Ann had made something of her face."[49] In this brief paragraph, O'Connor urges readers to complete the incomplete story.

The story *Why Do the Heathen Rage?* has been left incomplete, not only because of its author's sickness and premature death but also because O'Connor could not tell this particular story well at that time. Though a genius storyteller with deep insight into human nature, O'Connor knew her limits—she did not feel capable of entering the minds of Black characters. And *Why Do the Heathen Rage?* pushes that limitation: to tell the story of a white man who pretends to be Black without being able to understand the perspective of a Black person seems an ill-fated project. To finish her final novel, O'Connor required more time to reflect on the minds of her Black characters—Eustis, Alice, Roosevelt—and to consider Black as well as white readers, time that she did not receive.

As Alice Walker told her mother when they visited O'Connor's home, "The truth about any subject only comes when all the sides of the story are put together. . . . Each writer writes the missing parts to the other writer's story. And the whole story is what I'm after."[50] Walker acknowledges that the way forward is to bridge the divide between Black writers and white writers, between the marginalized and the elites, between the saints and the heathens. Walker refuses to accept a divided story, a segregated history, or a segregated literature. While Walker recognizes O'Connor's potential blind spots, rather than dismiss O'Connor's fiction, Walker steps up to fill in the rest, to gloss the original in order to illuminate the truth. If we are to be faithful readers, we should see the opportunity of this unfinished novel as a chance to do likewise.

AFTERWORD

Steve Prince, One Fish Studio

There is a mythical bird in Ghana called Sankofa. This bird moves forward while looking back. On one hand the act sounds irresponsible, but on the other hand we are jarred into understanding the beautiful, poetic nature of this creature's awareness of past, present, and future and the importance of passing it on. Artisans have rendered the bird with an egg in its beak, symbolically bespeaking of generations to come and our role in teaching and sharing the truth. *Sankofa* means "go back and fetch it," or operatively, those who forget their past are doomed to repeat it. In encountering Flannery O'Connor's words, I felt as if I were being transported in time before my birth while understanding clearly that the conditions that bore O'Connor, and her writing, offer an even clearer picture of who we were, who we are, who we are becoming, and dare I say, who we are constructed or imagined to be.

Conceiving illustrations to accompany this book was a fascinating journey. Stories, symbols, metaphors, and history are foundational to my artistic production. I recognized the absence or the invisibility of a true Black voice. The concept of simultaneity bubbled to the surface in my mind, and I was struck by some uncanny parallels with O'Connor's life and the life of Malcolm X. Flannery O'Connor and Malcolm X (Little) were born two months apart in 1925, and they both died prematurely before their fortieth birthday in 1964 and 1965, respectively. The contrast of these two individuals became the spark of my thinking of how to approach making art for this text. Each image is a sort of metanarrative: in one sense, to give flesh to the story that O'Connor is espousing, but in another sense to offer readers an additional narrative to embrace simultaneously. I attempt to give voice to the silence, the absence, the erased, the overlooked, the recesses, to encourage readers to embrace the fullness of our history during the period in which the text was written. O'Connor was able to live her last days writing on a farm in Georgia, eventually succumbing to complications surrounding lupus, whereas Malcolm X was slain by assassins' bullets while preaching in Audubon Ballroom in New York City.

I created seven linoleum cuts for the text. The image *Sticks and Stones* (page 21) alludes to the saying that "sticks and stones may break my bones, but words will never hurt me." I am not sure of the etymology of that saying, but Walter's words do hurt as he pecks away on his typewriter disguising himself as a Black man. I reflected on the historical constructions of Black men as predators of White women chronicled in seminal films like *Birth of a Nation* (1915) and the ways in which Black men were utilized as guinea pigs for the Tuskegee experiments stemming from the 1930s into the 1970s. What Walter creates reinforces the stereotypic constructions of Blackness and robs Black agency. Images flung from his typewriter help create constructions of reality.

The image *Chocolate Pie* (page 45) reveals Walter on his deathbed with his last words scribbled on a piece of paper beside him: "I, Walter . . ." Tilman enters the room carrying a piece of chocolate pie. Walter lies in a cruciform structure on the bed, as an echo to his imminent demise. I was struck by the idea of a chocolate pie; it is an offering of comfort in a painful season. What about the life of Roosevelt the servant, who serves every day until exhaustion and is never served? A miniature Black man stands on the plate beside the chocolate pie, unbeknownst to both White characters. He becomes a reminder to us to look with a deeper compassion for the Other. The pie signifies White privilege that oft times blindly moves and does not see the contributions of Black labor providing a space of comfort.

The image *Ancestral Water* (page 58) reflects a baptismal scene. A young Walter is being baptized by Mr. Simcox. Water is one of the most powerful Christian symbols. It is the substance that Christ transforms into wine, it is the substance that Christ walks on, it is the site of the spiritual rebirth that Christ teaches to Nicodemus, and it is the substance of which he tells the woman at the well she will "thirst no more" because he is "living water." With all the beautiful symbology that the Bible professes, somehow people have lost its meaning and packed human beings in wooden wombs, carried them for months, and deposited them in fields for centuries to build this nation. The water carries meaning, memory, and the tears of generations, and the ripples carry four ancestral faces who become overseers of this spiritual transformation. They bear witness to this momentous occasion, hoping that an epiphany of the spirit occurs. The trinity of telephone poles in the background reminds us of Golgotha and Christ's sacrifice.

The image *Unsung* (page 62) shows a disinterested Walter staring off into the distance while his mother chides him for not being more like Billie Watts. Watts is pictured above the fold on the 4-H newspaper with his prize-winning Duroc hog. His mother wonders if she raised him right. I wondered about the unsung heroes who marched for equality and those who fought for voting rights. I wondered about those men who dangled from trees like strange fruit, and I wondered about four innocent little girls with pigtails whose flame was exterminated in the basement of Sixteenth Street Baptist Church in 1963. I contemplated the priorities and the things we deem to be important.

The image *Letterhead* (page 80) reeks of the structure of a romance novel. Our protagonist sits upon a rock in the forest among the whistling trees, reading a passionate letter from Oona Gibbs. The four trees flanking Walter are subtle reminders of the four Gospels and the hope that he will awake from this living nightmare of posing as a

Black man in his written response to Oona. Walter sits in blackface in step with the history of minstrelsy in our nation that stemmed from the early 1800s to the twentieth century. The problematic and damaging nature of this ruse is a reminder of the power of representation or the lack thereof and the stains that are embedded in the fabric of America that we must collectively clean.

The image *Presumption of Knowing* (page 96) shows Walter sitting on a chair with his hand outstretched and two Black people resting there with fists upraised expressing Black Power and a cry for equality. "Each man is an island unto himself," the saying goes. Or should I rather say each person is a carrier of generations? Do we look at each other with a presumptive gaze, or do we open the doors of our castle and allow others to truly enter, and vice versa? The piece reminds us of the importance of seeing each other and not creating or reifying damaging constructions that render our personal space more valuable or important than that of our neighbor.

The image *See Me* (page 120) reveals a marching Oona Gibbs denouncing her wealth and committing her life to feel, understand, and live the life of the oppressed and marginalized. She wears her sandals and peasant skirt while being flanked by protesters taking it to the streets. Noble and naive, she sets out on a journey to right wrongs; she bears her cross. Paper flutters to the ground, reminding us that we are a living letter, a living epistle.

ABOUT THE ILLUSTRATOR

Steve Prince, artist, educator, art evangelist

Steve Prince is a native of New Orleans, Louisiana, and currently resides in Williamsburg, Virginia. He received his BFA from Xavier University of Louisiana and his MFA in printmaking and sculpture from Michigan State University. He is the director of engagement and distinguished artist in residence at the Muscarelle Museum of Art at William and Mary University. Prince is a member of the national honor society Omicron Delta Kappa for his leadership and service. He is an educator with over twenty-five years of experience in teaching middle school, high school, and college. He has created several public and private commissions nationally, including a ten-foot bronze sculpture titled *Sankofa Seed* at William and Mary University, and a fifteen-foot stainless steel sculpture titled *Song for John* for the city of Hampton, Virginia. He has received numerous honors for his art and scholarship, including the 2020 International Engage Art Contest Visual Art Grand Prize Winner, the VMFA Artist Fellowship, and the 2010 Teacher of the Year for the City of Hampton. Prince has shown his art internationally in various solo, group, and juried exhibitions.

Prince is an accomplished international lecturer and workshop conductor, using a variety of media. In 2019 he worked with over five hundred people to create a collective art piece focusing on the history of chattel slavery stemming from the first documented Africans arriving on the shores of Point Comfort in 1619. His project was called Links which metaphorically championed the inextricable connections we have as human beings. Prince spreads a message of hope and renewal to the global community. His philosophy is derived from the cathartic jazz funerary tradition in New Orleans, called the dirge and second line. Conversely, the dirge represents the everyday issues and pains we confront and endure, whereas the second line represents new life, restoration, salvation, and yearning for the eternal while we are still alive.

NOTES

Introduction

1. Sally Fitzgerald records this story in Flannery O'Connor, *The Habit of Being: The Letters of Flannery O'Connor*, ed. Sally Fitzgerald (New York: Farrar, Straus & Giroux, 1979), 22.

2. O'Connor, letter to Betty Boyd Love, December 23, 1950, in *Habit of Being*, 22.

3. The following details are drawn from Brad Gooch, *Flannery: A Life of Flannery O'Connor* (New York: Little, Brown, 2009), chap. 6 ("The Life You Save").

4. Flannery O'Connor, "Good Country People," in *The Complete Stories* (New York: Farrar, Straus & Giroux, 1990), 276.

5. Stuart Burns, "How Wide Did 'The Heathen' Rage?," *Flannery O'Connor Bulletin* 4 (1975): 26.

6. Marian Burns, "The Chronology of Flannery O'Connor's *Why Do the Heathen Rage?*," *Flannery O'Connor Bulletin* 11 (1982): 73.

7. In addition to Stuart Burns and Marian Burns, Virginia Wray published "Flannery O'Connor's *Why Do the Heathen Rage?* and the Quotidian 'Larger Things,'" *Flannery O'Connor Bulletin* 23 (1994–95): 1–29. These three articles made up the majority of scholarship on the manuscripts from 1970 to 1995. However, in 2015, Colleen Warren published "Seeing Potential in the Heathen: Flannery O'Connor's Unfinished Novel," *Flannery O'Connor Review* 13 (2015): 105–22; and M. K. Shaddix discussed the manuscripts in detail in her book *The Church without the Church: Desert Orthodoxy in Flannery's Dear Old Dirty Southland* (Macon, GA: Mercer University Press, 2015). My own contribution to the criticism may be found in "O'Connor's Unfinished Novel: The Beginning of a Modern Saint's Life," in *Revelation and Convergence: Flannery O'Connor and the Catholic Intellectual Tradition*, ed. Mark Bosco and Brent Little (Washington, DC: Catholic University of America Press, 2017), 191–214.

8. Flannery O'Connor, "Why Do the Heathen Rage?" (unpublished manuscript, Georgia College and State University Special Collections), folder 215.

9. Flannery O'Connor, "Everything That Rises Must Converge," in *Collected Works* (New York: Penguin, 1988), 500.

10. Flannery O'Connor, "Why Do the Heathens Rage?," *Esquire*, July 1, 1963, https://classic.esquire.com/article/1963/7/1/why-do-the-heathens-rage.

11. O'Connor, letter to John Hawkes, September 10, 1963, in *Habit of Being*, 537.

12. O'Connor, "Why Do the Heathen Rage?," folder 228a.32.

13. Benny Andrews, afterword to Flannery O'Connor, *Everything That Rises Must Converge*, etchings by Benny Andrews (New York: Limited Editions Club, 2005). This book is a stand-alone illustrated edition of the short story.

Why Do the Heathen Rage? The Porch Scene

1. Flannery O'Connor, "Why Do the Heathen Rage?" (unpublished manuscript, Georgia College and State University Special Collections), folders 220b.1–2; 220c.1; 220d.1; 220e.1; 221.1; 222.2–16, 22; 223.1–16, 20–22; 224.1–16, 20–21; 229a.1.

Koinonia

1. Flannery O'Connor, letter to Betty Hester, May 18, 1957, in O'Connor, *The Habit of Being: The Letters of Flannery O'Connor*, ed. Sally Fitzgerald (New York: Farrar, Straus & Giroux, 1979), 219–20.

2. O'Connor, letter to Betty Hester, May 4, 1957, in *Habit of Being*, 218.

3. Flannery O'Connor, "Why Do the Heathen Rage?" (unpublished manuscript, Georgia College and State University Special Collections), folders 216, 217.

4. O'Connor, "Why Do the Heathen Rage?," folders 222, 223, 224.

5. O'Connor, "Why Do the Heathen Rage?," folders 222, 226, 227, 228.

6. Charles Marsh recounts how Jordan had to explain to Citizens' Councils "the difference between Jesus and Marx, hoping to reassure the group that he was a follower of the former not the latter." Marsh, *The Beloved Community: How Faith Shapes Social Justice, from the Civil Rights Movement to Today* (New York: Basic Books, 2005), 76.

7. Marsh, *Beloved Community*, 73.

Sequel to "The Enduring Chill"

1. Flannery O'Connor, letter to Maryat Lee, February 1957, in O'Connor, *The Habit of Being: The Letters of Flannery O'Connor*, ed. Sally Fitzgerald (New York: Farrar, Straus & Giroux, 1979), 203.

2. O'Connor, letter to "A," February 4, 1961, in *Habit of Being*, 30.

3. The phrase "long obedience in the same direction" comes from Friedrich Nietzsche, *Beyond Good and Evil* 5.188, trans. Helen Zimmern, in *The Complete Works of Friedrich Nietzsche* (1909–1913), available at https://www.gutenberg.org/files/4363/4363-h/4363 -h.htm. Eugene Peterson draws on this phrase in the title of his book *A Long Obedience in the Same Direction: Discipleship in an Instant Society* (Downers Grove, IL: InterVarsity, 2019).

4. O'Connor, letter to Sister Mariella Gable, May 4, 1963, in *Habit of Being*, 518.

5. O'Connor, letter to Betty Hester, December 28, 1957, in *Habit of Being*, 261.

6. O'Connor, letter to Ted Spivey, October 19, 1958, in *Habit of Being*, 299.

7. O'Connor, letter to Maryat Lee, May 6, 1959, in *Habit of Being*, 331.

8. O'Connor, letter to Cecil Dawkins, November 8, 1963, in *Habit of Being*, 546.

9. In May 2017 a fellow at GCSU library, James Owen, gave me a tour around Milledgeville that included walking through the cemetery and pointing out gravestones that share names with O'Connor characters.

10. A colleague of mine, Steve Porter at Biola University, pointed out the similarity to Walter Hilton and uncovered the review by O'Connor.

11. "He told her [his mother] that he was a secular contemplative." Flannery O'Connor, "Why Do the Heathen Rage?" (unpublished manuscript, Georgia College and State University Special Collections), folder 226b.26.

12. O'Connor, letter to J. F. Powers, December 9, 1956, in *Habit of Being*, 185.

13. O'Connor, letter to J. F. Powers, December 9, 1956, in *Habit of Being*, 190.

14. O'Connor, "Why Do the Heathen Rage?," folder 234.65.

Why Do the Heathen Rage? Walter's Last Will and Testament

1. Flannery O'Connor, "Why Do the Heathen Rage?" (unpublished manuscript, Georgia College and State University Special Collections), folder 232a.41–49.

2. This paragraph has been added by the author to help with narrative flow.

3. Flannery O'Connor, interview with C. Ross Mullins Jr., *Jubilee* 11 (June 1963): 32–35, reprinted in *Conversations with Flannery O'Connor*, ed. Rosemary Magee (Jackson: University of Mississippi Press, 1987), 107.

4. Flannery O'Connor, "The Enduring Chill," in *The Complete Stories* (New York: Farrar, Straus & Giroux, 1990), 370.

5. O'Connor, "Why Do the Heathen Rage?," folder 231a.33.

6. O'Connor, "Good Country People," in *Complete Stories*, 291.

7. Flannery O'Connor, "Novelist and Believer," in O'Connor, *Mystery and Manners*, ed. Sally Fitzgerald and Robert Fitzgerald (New York: Farrar, Straus & Giroux, 1969), 161.

8. O'Connor, "Why Do the Heathen Rage?," folder 226a.27.

Why Do the Heathen Rage? Baptism

1. Flannery O'Connor, "Why Do the Heathen Rage?" (unpublished manuscript, Georgia College and State University Special Collections), folder 233.58.

2. O'Connor, "Why Do the Heathen Rage?," folder 232c.26.

3. "Interview with C. Ross Mullins Jr.," *Jubilee* 11 (June 1963): 32–35, in Rosemary Magee, ed., *Conversations with Flannery O'Connor* (Jackson: University of Mississippi Press, 1987), 104.

4. Flannery O'Connor, letter to "A," January 17, 1956, in O'Connor, *The Habit of Being: The Letters of Flannery O'Connor*, ed. Sally Fitzgerald (New York: Farrar, Straus & Giroux, 1979), 131.

5. O'Connor, letter to Robert Jiras, August 28, 1956, Emory University Archives, Atlanta, Georgia, manuscript collection no. 1305, series 1 ("Correspondence, 1925–1965, 2004"), box 39, https://findingaids.library.emory.edu/documents/oconnor1305.

6. Flannery O'Connor, "The River," in *Collected Works* (New York: Library of America, 1984), 165.

7. Flannery O'Connor, "The Nature and Aim of Fiction," in O'Connor, *Mystery and Manners*, ed. Sally Fitzgerald and Robert Fitzgerald (New York: Farrar, Straus & Giroux, 1969), 81.

8. When scholar Marian Burns investigated the holdings at Georgia College and State University, she noted that a two-page manuscript, number 194a (then labeled 186a), began as a sequel to "The Enduring Chill" and thus should belong to the *Why Do the Heathen Rage?* manuscripts: "It is clearly the next chapter of a projected novel, or sequence of short stories, about Asbury, inspired by the story already published." Burns, "The Chronology of Flannery O'Connor's *Why Do the Heathen Rage?*," *Flannery O'Connor Bulletin* 11 (1982): 63.

Why Do the Heathen Rage? Walter/Asbury's Childhood

1. Flannery O'Connor, "Why Do the Heathen Rage?" (unpublished manuscript, Georgia College and State University Special Collections), folder 194a.1–2.

2. Flannery O'Connor, introduction to *A Memoir of Mary Ann*, in *Collected Works* (New York: Library of America, 1984), 822.

Why Do the Heathen Rage? Walter Recites the Ten Commandments

1. Flannery O'Connor, "Why Do the Heathen Rage?" (unpublished manuscript, Georgia College and State University Special Collections), folder 225e.23–24.

2. "The writer has to make corruption believable before he can make the grace meaningful." O'Connor, letter to Sister Mariella Gable, May 4, 1963, in O'Connor, *The Habit of Being: The Letters of Flannery O'Connor*, ed. Sally Fitzgerald (New York: Farrar, Straus & Giroux, 1979), 516.

3. Ross Douthat, *Bad Religion: How We Became a Nation of Heretics* (New York: Free Press, 2012).

4. Elizabeth Gilbert, *Eat, Pray, Love: One Woman's Search for Everything across Italy, India and Indonesia* (New York: Viking, 2006), 122.

5. Flannery O'Connor, "Greenleaf," in *Collected Works* (New York: Library of America, 1984), 506.

6. Flannery O'Connor, "The Teaching of Literature," in *Mystery and Manners*, ed. Sally Fitzgerald and Robert Fitzgerald (New York: Farrar, Straus & Giroux, 1969), 124.

7. O'Connor, letter to Rev. Kirkland, January 19, 1963, in response to January 17, 1963, in Emory University Archives, Atlanta, Georgia, manuscript collection no. 1305, series 1 ("Correspondence, 1925–1965, 2004"), box 6, folder 7, https://findingaids.library.emory.edu/documents/oconnor1305.

8. Reading these comments, Ralph Wood pointed out this distinction.

9. O'Connor, letter to Robert Giroux, November 1962, in *Habit of Being*, 498.

Epistolary Blackface

1. Flannery O'Connor, "Why Do the Heathen Rage?" (unpublished manuscript, Georgia College and State University Special Collections), folders 222.24; 228.21.

2. O'Connor, "Why Do the Heathen Rage?," folder 228a.30.

3. Flannery O'Connor, letter to J. H. McCown, October 28, 1960, in O'Connor, *The Habit of Being: The Letters of Flannery O'Connor*, ed. Sally Fitzgerald (New York: Farrar, Straus & Giroux, 1979), 414.

4. O'Connor, letter to Maryat Lee, May 21, 1964, in *Habit of Being*, 580.

5. Walker Percy, *The Last Gentleman* (New York: Picador, 1966), 130.

6. O'Connor, "Why Do the Heathen Rage?," folders 218a.6; 226a.18; 226.19; 228a.25.

7. "An Interview with Flannery O'Connor: Katherine Fugin, Faye Rivard, and Margaret Sieh," *Censer* (College of St. Teresa, Winona, Minnesota) (Fall 1960): 28–30, reprinted in *Conversations with Flannery O'Connor*, ed. Rosemary Magee (Jackson: University of Mississippi Press, 1987), 59.

8. Twain's words are from his letters to the San Francisco newspaper *Alta California* (August 1, 1869), quoted in Tyehimba Jess, *Olio* (Seattle: Wave Books, 2016), 18.

9. Dan Wanschura, "The Unconventional Poetry of Tyehimba Jess," NPR, July 15, 2017, https://www.npr.org/2017/07/15/537381252/the-unconventional-poetry-of-tyehimba-jess.

10. Tyehimba Jess, "Pre/Face Berryman/Brown," in Jess, *Olio*, 73.

11. Berryman even called Ralph Ellison repeatedly, requesting that he read drafts of the songs and provide feedback, according to Paul Mariani, *Dream Song: The Life of John Berryman* (San Antonio: Trinity University Press, 1990), 387.

12. Dorothy L. Sayers, "Are Women Human?," *A Matter of Eternity: Selections from the Writings of Dorothy L. Sayers*, ed. Rosamond Kent Sprague (Grand Rapids: Eerdmans, 1973), 34.

13. Hilton Als, "This Lonesome Place," *New Yorker*, January 21, 2001, https://www .newyorker.com/magazine/2001/01/29/this-lonesome-place.

14. Clint Smith, *How the Word Is Passed: A Reckoning with the History of Slavery across America* (New York: Little, Brown, 2021), 289.

15. Mark Twain, *Adventures of Huckleberry Finn*, ed. Alan Gribben (Montgomery, AL: NewSouth Books, 2012).

16. Jon Swaine, "Censored Huckleberry Finn Prompts Political Correctness Debate," *The Telegraph*, January 5, 2011, https://www.telegraph.co.uk/news/worldnews/northameri ca/usa/8239737/Censored-Huckleberry-Finn-prompts-political-correctness-debate.html.

17. John McWhorter, "How the N-Word Became Unsayable," *New York Times*, April 30, 2021, https://www.nytimes.com/2021/04/30/opinion/john-mcwhorter-n-word-unsayable.html.

18. Randall Kennedy, *Nigger: The Strange Career of a Troublesome Word* (New York: Pantheon, 2002).

19. Ann Oldenburg, "Oprah: 'You Cannot Be My Friend' and Use N-word," *USA Today*, July 31, 2013, https://www.usatoday.com/story/life/people/2013/07/31/oprah-you-cannot-b e-my-friend-and-use-n-word/2604587.

20. Ta-Nehisi Coates, "In Defense of a Loaded Word," *New York Times*, November 23, 2013, https://www.nytimes.com/2013/11/24/opinion/sunday/coates-in-defense-of-a-loaded -word.html.

21. Alan Jacobs, *Breaking Bread with the Dead: A Guide to a Tranquil Mind* (New York: Penguin, 2020), 55.

Why Do the Heathen Rage? The Black Double

1. Flannery O'Connor, "Why Do the Heathen Rage?" (unpublished manuscript, Georgia College and State University Special Collections), folders 222.23–29; 226a.15–18; 226c.16–20; 228a.20–30.

Maryat Lee and Oona Gibbs

1. Flannery O'Connor, letter to Maryat Lee, January 9, 1957, in O'Connor, *The Habit of Being: The Letters of Flannery O'Connor*, ed. Sally Fitzgerald (New York: Farrar, Straus & Giroux, 1979), 195.

2. James Lewis McLeod, *Flannery O'Connor and Me: The Friendship between Flannery and Me* (Xlibris, 2017), 103.

3. Maryat Lee, letter to Flannery O'Connor, August 22, 1958 (Georgia College and State University Special Collections).

4. Maryat Lee, letter to Flannery O'Connor, April 24, 1960, quoted in Sarah Gordon, "Maryat and Julian and the 'Not so Bloodless Revolution,'" *Flannery O'Connor Bulletin* 21 (1992): 25–36.

5. Gordon, "Maryat," 32.

6. From Maryat's journal, dated 1965, quoted in Jean W. Cash, "Maryat and 'Flanneryat': An Antithetical Friendship," *Flannery O'Connor Bulletin* 19 (1990): 56.

7. McLeod, *Flannery O'Connor and Me*, 108.

8. Fitzgerald, in O'Connor, *Habit of Being*, 193–94.

9. Colleen Warren, "Seeing Potential in the Heathen: Flannery O'Connor's Unfinished Novel," *Flannery O'Connor Review* 13 (2015): 117.

10. O'Connor, letter to Maryat Lee, June 9, 1957, in *Habit of Being*, 224.

11. Maryat Lee, letter to Flannery O'Connor, June 24, 1957, from Japan (Georgia College and State University Special Collections).

12. Brad Gooch, *Flannery: A Life of Flannery O'Connor* (New York: Little, Brown, 2009), 293.

Documenting "Real" Life

1. Flannery O'Connor, letter to "A," August 17, 1963, in O'Connor, *The Habit of Being: The Letters of Flannery O'Connor*, ed. Sally Fitzgerald (New York: Farrar, Straus & Giroux, 1979), 534.

2. Flannery O'Connor, "Why Do the Heathen Rage?" (unpublished manuscript, Georgia College and State University Special Collections), folder 232e.41.

3. O'Connor, "Why Do the Heathen Rage?," folder 228a.36–40.

Why Do the Heathen Rage? Photo Journal

1. Flannery O'Connor, "Why Do the Heathen Rage?" (unpublished manuscript, Georgia College and State University Special Collections), folder 228a.30–42.

The Revolting Conversion

1. Flannery O'Connor, "Why Do the Heathen Rage?" (unpublished manuscript, Georgia College and State University Special Collections), folder 226f.30.

2. For this and the following revisions, see O'Connor, "Why Do the Heathen Rage?," folders 220a.1; 220b.1; 220c.1; 220d.1; 220e.1; 221.1; 223.1; 224.1; 229a.1; 229b.1; 229c.1; 229d.1.

3. O'Connor, letter to Andrew Lytle, February 4, 1960, in Flannery O'Connor, *The Habit of Being: The Letters of Flannery O'Connor*, ed. Sally Fitzgerald (New York: Farrar, Straus & Giroux, 1979), 373.

4. C. S. Lewis, *Surprised by Joy* (New York: Harcourt, Brace, Jovanovich, 1966), 290.

5. O'Connor, "Why Do the Heathen Rage?," folders 222.29; 226a.19; 226b.21; 226e.21.

Why Do the Heathen Rage? Do Not Come, Oona Gibbs!

1. Flannery O'Connor, "Why Do the Heathen Rage?" (unpublished manuscript, Georgia College and State University Special Collections), folders 218a.7–9; 218d.6; 218e.9; 226a.20–27; 226b.29–30; 226f.27–31; 227c.10; 226e.22; 224.21.

Why Do the Heathen Rage? The Girl

1. Flannery O'Connor, "Why Do the Heathen Rage?" (unpublished manuscript, Georgia College and State University Special Collections), folders 229a.1–8; 229b.1–4; 229c.1–2; 229d.1; 229e.1; 230a.8–12; 230b.8–10; 230c.10.

Who Is Oona Gibbs? Mother, Daughter, Aunt, Cousin, or Lover

1. Flannery O'Connor, "Why Do the Heathen Rage?" (unpublished manuscript, Georgia College and State University Special Collections), folder 228a.3.

2. Flannery O'Connor, introduction to *A Memoir of Mary Ann*, in O'Connor, *Mystery and Manners*, ed. Sally Fitzgerald and Robert Fitzgerald (New York: Farrar, Straus & Giroux, 1969), 227.

3. Flannery O'Connor, letter to "A," April 27, 1963, in O'Connor, *The Habit of Being: The Letters of Flannery O'Connor*, ed. Sally Fitzgerald (New York: Farrar, Straus & Giroux, 1979), 515.

4. Fyodor Dostoevsky, *The Brothers Karamazov*, trans. Constance Garnett (New York: Norton, 1976), 616.

5. Marian Burns argues that the aunt section must have been written around 1963 because of an overlap between the aunt's "dear old dirty Southland" and O'Connor's use of the identical phrase in a letter to Hester (September 1, 1963); yet Burns overlooks the fact that O'Connor used this phrase multiple times in her letters, including as early as 1958 in a letter to Maryat Lee. O'Connor, *Habit of Being*, 266.

Why Do the Heathen Rage? Walter's Aunt

1. Flannery O'Connor, "Why Do the Heathen Rage?" (unpublished manuscript, Georgia College and State University Special Collections), folder 231b.5–6.

2. O'Connor, "Why Do the Heathen Rage?," folder 232a.46.

3. Sarah Gordon, *Flannery O'Connor: The Obedient Imagination* (Athens: University of Georgia Press, 2003), 246.

Burning Crosses

1. "Cross Burned at Home of G.S.C.W. President," *Atlanta Constitution*, cited in Patrick Novotny, *This Georgia Rising: Education, Civil Rights, and the Politics of Change in Georgia in the 1940s* (Macon, GA: Mercer University Press, 2007), 309n415.

2. Maryat Lee, letter to Flannery O'Connor, January 26, 1957 (Georgia College and State University Special Collections).

The Violent Bear It Away: The Burnt Cross

1. Flannery O'Connor, "The Violent Bear It Away" (unpublished manuscript, Georgia College and State University Special Collections), folders 160–65.

Why Do the Heathen Rage? One Potential Ending

1. James Cone, *The Cross and the Lynching Tree* (Maryknoll, NY: Orbis Books, 2011), 13.

2. Countee Cullen, "The Black Christ," in *The Black Christ and Other Poems* (New York: Harper & Brothers, 1929), 69.

3. Angela Alaimo O'Donnell, *Andalusian Hours: Poems from the Porch of Flannery O'Connor* (Brewster, MA: Paraclete, 2020), 10.

4. Michael Pietsch, "Editor's Note," in David Foster Wallace, *The Pale King* (New York: Little, Brown, 2011), ix–x.

5. Julian of Norwich, *Revelations of Divine Love*, chap. 51, trans. Elizabeth Spearing (New York: Penguin, 1999).

6. Flannery O'Connor, *Wise Blood*, 2nd ed. (New York: Farrar, Straus & Giroux, 1962).

7. Flannery O'Connor, *The Violent Bear It Away*, in *Collected Works* (New York: Library of America, 1984), 479.

8. O'Connor, "The Enduring Chill," in *The Complete Stories* (New York: Farrar, Straus & Giroux, 1990), 377.

9. Flannery O'Connor, letter to Maryat Lee, August, 17, 1962, in O'Connor, *The Habit of Being: The Letters of Flannery O'Connor*, ed. Sally Fitzgerald (New York: Farrar, Straus & Giroux, 1979), 489.

10. Toni Morrison, *Playing in the Dark: Whiteness and the Literary Imagination* (New York: Vintage, 1993), 18.

The Other Half of the Story

1. Brad Gooch, *Flannery: A Life of Flannery O'Connor* (New York: Little, Brown, 2009), 67; "Biographical Information on Flannery O'Connor," Georgia College Library (website), last updated June 21, 2022, https://libguides.gcsu.edu/oconnor-bio/FAQ.

2. Flannery O'Connor, "A Late Encounter with the Enemy," in *Collected Works* (New York: Library of America, 1984), 254.

3. *Gone with the Wind*, directed by Victor Fleming (1939; Selznick International Pictures and Metro-Goldwyn-Mayer).

4. W. J. Cash, *The Mind of the South* (New York: Vintage, 1960), 8.

5. Cash, *Mind of the South*, 20.

6. Flannery O'Connor, letter to Louise Abbot, January 13, 1961, in O'Connor, *The Habit of Being: The Letters of Flannery O'Connor*, ed. Sally Fitzgerald (New York: Farrar, Straus & Giroux, 1979), 426.

7. O'Connor, "The Enduring Chill," in *Collected Works*, 560.

8. Walker Percy, quoted in Jay Tolson, *Pilgrim in the Ruins: A Life of Walker Percy* (New York: Simon & Schuster, 1992), 298.

9. Flannery O'Connor, "The Regional Writer," in O'Connor, *Mystery and Manners*, ed. Sally Fitzgerald and Robert Fitzgerald (New York: Farrar, Straus & Giroux, 1969), 59.

10. O'Connor, "The Fiction Writer and His Country," in *Mystery and Manners*, 35.

11. Alice Walker, *In Search of Our Mothers' Gardens: Womanist Prose* (San Diego: Harcourt Brace Jovanovich, 1983), 48.

12. Walker, *In Search of Our Mothers' Gardens*, 49.

13. Marian Burns, "O'Connor's Unfinished Novel," in *Critical Essays on Flannery O'Connor*, ed. Beverly Lyon Clark and Melvin J. Friedman (Boston: G. K. Hall, 1985), 169–80.

14. Virginia Wray, "Flannery O'Connor's 'Why Do the Heathen Rage?' and the Quotidian 'Larger Things,'" *Flannery O'Connor Bulletin* 23 (1994–95): 3, https://www.jstor.org/stable/26670322.

15. Wray, "Flannery O'Connor's 'Why Do the Heathen Rage?,'" 3.

16. Flannery O'Connor, *A Prayer Journal*, ed. W. A. Sessions (New York: Farrar, Straus & Giroux, 2013), 4.

17. O'Connor, "Catholic Novelists and Their Readers," in *Mystery and Manners*, 179.

18. Walter Brueggemann, *The Prophetic Imagination*, 40th anniv. ed. (Minneapolis: Fortress, 2018), xiv.

19. O'Connor, "Catholic Novelists and Their Readers," in *Mystery and Manners*, 179.

20. O'Connor, "A Good Man Is Hard to Find," in *Collected Works*, 149–50.

21. Brueggemann, *Prophetic Imagination*, 3.

22. Toni Morrison, *Playing in the Dark: Whiteness and the Literary Imagination* (New York: Vintage, 1993); O'Connor, "The Artificial N——," in *Collected Works*, 210.

23. O'Connor, "The Artificial N——," in *Collected Works*, 265.

24. Flannery O'Connor, letter to Ben Griffith, May 4, 1955, in O'Connor, *Habit of Being*, 78.

25. O'Connor, "The Artificial N——," in *Collected Works*, 269.

26. O'Connor, "The Artificial N——," in *Collected Works*, 270.

27. Toni Morrison, *The Origin of Others* (Cambridge, MA: Harvard University Press, 2017), 23.

28. Morrison, *Origin of Others*, 23.

29. Clint Smith, *How the Word Is Passed: A Reckoning with the History of Slavery across America* (New York: Little, Brown, 2021), 286.

30. Morrison, *Origin of Others*, 21.

31. Margaret Earley Whitt, "The Pivotal Year, 1963: Flannery O'Connor and the Civil Rights Movement," in *Political Companion to Flannery O'Connor*, ed. Henry T. Edmondson (Lexington: University Press of Kentucky, 2017), 60.

32. National Museum of American History, "Summer of 1963," accessed June 3, 2023, https://americanhistory.si.edu/changing-america-emancipation-proclamation-1863-and -march-washington-1963/1963/summer-1963-0.

33. Whitt, "Pivotal Year," 70.

34. O'Connor, letter to Maryat Lee, May 21, 1964, in *Habit of Being*, 580.

35. O'Connor, introduction to *A Memoir of Mary Ann*, in *Mystery and Manners*, 227.

36. Paul Elie, "How Racist Was Flannery O'Connor?," *New Yorker*, June 15, 2020, https:// www.newyorker.com/magazine/2020/06/22/how-racist-was-flannery-oconnor.

37. Comments from a student petition: "Get Loyola to Rename Flannery O'Connor Residence Hall," Change.org, accessed April 26, 2023, https://www.change.org/p/loyola -university-maryland-get-loyola-to-rename-flannery-o-connor-residence-hall.

38. Alan Jacobs, *Breaking Bread with the Dead* (New York: Penguin, 2020), 55.

39. "Southern Writers Are Stuck with the South," *Atlanta Magazine* 3 (August 1963): 26, 60, 63, in *Conversations with Flannery O'Connor*, ed. Rosemary Magee (Jackson: University of Mississippi Press, 1987), 109.

40. O'Connor, letter to Cecil Dawkins, November 5, 1963, in *Habit of Being*, 546.

41. Some of these paragraphs were published in Jessica Hooten Wilson, "How Flannery O'Connor Fought Racism," *First Things*, June 24, 2020, in response to Elie, "How Racist Was Flannery O'Connor?"

42. O'Connor, "Revelation," in *Collected Works*, 642.

43. O'Connor, "Revelation," in *The Complete Stories* (New York: Farrar, Straus & Giroux, 1990), 500.

44. O'Connor, "Revelation," in *Collected Works*, 654.

45. O'Connor, letter to Maryat Lee, cited in Elie, "How Racist Was Flannery O'Connor?"

46. Elie, "How Racist Was Flannery O'Connor?"

47. O'Connor, "Novelist and Believer," in *Mystery and Manners*, 168.

48. O'Connor, letter to Janet McKane, July 8, 1964, in *Habit of Being*, 591: "I also had him give me the now called Sacrament of the Sick. Once known as Extreme Unction."

49. O'Connor, introduction to *A Memoir of Mary Ann*, in *Mystery and Manners*, 223.

50. Walker, *In Search of Our Mothers' Gardens*, 49.